HALF-NATTY

FREDDY FOX

For York

Some names have been changed.
Some haven't.

NEWBIE

Someone kept a diary during *The Great Fire of London* so girls might read about the fire in my pants and wish they'd been around.

Right now the only girl calling is my mother. She's dumped dad, says it's a crisis, and wants me back from uni. It's Valentine's Day and I'm asked to hug a man.

Got no cards (postal strike) but the student paper arrived with the headline BIEBER! BABES! BRITAIN! It has a photo of him flexing his physique. Can't he afford a shirt? We have the same birthday coming up. I'm 19 years from being a 40-year-old virgin. Doubt he is. He'd do himself if he could. He has a live Q & A on YouTube later. I'd never watch YouTube.

If I built my body, what would Bieber or any male have over me?

SUN 15 FEB

7 p.m. On the train home with no signal so reading the student paper. Bieber's over here promoting himself and says he likes British "babes". Where are these babes? Why haven't they seen me? The girl opposite hasn't seen me. She's staring at Bieber's bulges.

11 p.m. Arrived back at the Fox-hole. Sister and dad asleep. Crisis? It can't be a crisis if people are snoring. I really hate Sundays. Sundays remind me of school the next day. Going to bed, by myself.

MON 16 FEB

Sister banged on my door first thing asking to borrow the student paper. Hasn't she got enough to read in a library? She's like the girl on the train, fooled by photos. I'd never be fooled by photos.

Dad's off work dealing with being dumped and watches cartoons. Is this where I get half my brains from? Must find out how long I'm needed as the new semester starts soon. Dad's not speaking so I'll ask alleged sister when she gets in from work.

Started a plan to do push-ups every day. Did 20 in total and it only took 6 attempts. I'm a quick learner so by the time I go back to uni I'll do 100 non-stop then no girl will ignore me. Or my bulges.

6 p.m. Sister back and insisting questions start with her name. Gave in. "Alexa, how long am I needed here?" Alexa can't answer that query but she'll contact our missing mother to find out. I'll contact Jeff Bezos to suggest he re-brands his devices.

TUE 17 FEB
PANCAKE DAY

Mother refuses to return and now doesn't "need a man". This is what happens when wi-fi reaches the kitchen. Why can't sister help? Her library job's part-time and her college is online. Tourism isn't even a proper subject. At least my degree in English will have guaranteed career prospects.

Did push-ups again but only got 10. Why am I half the man I was yesterday? This place weakens me. And I'm feeling pains somewhere. Could be the stress.

No parents, no pancakes, no calories, no care.

WED 18 FEB

Chest and arms hurt, poisoned by dad's cooking. If I die now I won't know what it feels like to have the love of a woman. Must stay alive. For them also.

Mother texted to say dad's unable to light her fires. I felt ill but it got worse. She asked if I could "pause" my studies. Pause? Is my destiny a download? She said dad's falling apart because he depended on a woman. Why have I never depended on a woman? Told her my studies were important and she cried. She said it's a chance to be the man of the family. Thought we already had one. What a Fox-up.

THU 19 FEB
CHINESE NEW YEAR

Chinese New Year so I've put on red socks as red's lucky. No one does fashion in the Fox-hole. Dad stumbles around shirt-free and shame-free in his boxers.

Course leader says I can delay uni for two weeks but any more time away and I'll have to repeat. Dad better snap out of feeling sorry for himself. I'd never feel sorry for myself.

Chest feels bruised inside and sister refuses to cook. Her attitude explains the lack of famous female chefs.

Looked up the origin of Bieber. German for *beaver*.

FRI 20 FEB

Had weird dream. Someone was holding a yellow paper ticket with *Spectator ONLY* on it. This happened for real whenever we collected sister from swimming lessons. Mother handed me one as sister swum and I spectated. What if I fell off a boat?

Dad strolled back into his job at *Terrific Tours* and told customers "Don't travel anywhere there's a woman." The manager dragged him out. He came home cocky then watched cartoons. I fear the worst.

SAT 21 FEB

The worst arrived. The manager phoned and fired dad. I warned him about handling words with care. Bet I end up stuck here now. Meanwhile according to the news, Bieber's jetted off. How is that news? When will I jet off?

Went for a think-walk and saw no babes. Bet they've jetted-off with Beaver. Felt better when I glanced in an electrical store window. They had a camera which filmed the street and showed it on all the TVs. My chest looks good on camera. Girls will soon notice it in real life. After a few seconds I saw staff noticing me noticing myself. Made me realize how stressful fame is. I might choose to be an unfamous poet.

SUN 22 FEB

Felt dumb being away from uni so I went into the loft to stimulate mind. Found my old 1000-piece *World Map* jigsaw.

It was almost perfect but had a bit missing. I took this as a metaphor. Picked up a kid's book on ancient civilizations. Their statues look like *Marvel* before *Marvel*. The ancients thought a good body was important as a good mind. As my mind is already superior I'll start a proper regime, not just push-ups. Then I'll be a perfect man instead of a partial puzzle. Told sister and she reckons I should get a program online. For someone who works in a library that's pretty dumb. All of life's problems are solved by cracking the alphabet. Asked her to get me some books.

Mother called after dad got fired. Thought she changed her mind about coming back but she just said to be the man he never was. Forgot to ask in which way.

MON 23 FEB

8 a.m. Heard dad say "Love yourself, don't wait." He's lost it. Spoke to uni who say I need proof to "pause" my course. Offered to put dad on the phone but they want a note. Will visit doctor to act depressed. Should be easy.

6 p.m. Doctor gave me a note to confirm my madness and I emailed it to uni. Heart went wrong after hit *Send*. If I die this diary will explain everything: *Freddy Fox was killed by his own kindness*. I'm now a temporary dropout who looks permanently retarded on paper.

Sister came home without training books. Told her she promised and she shouted "IT CAN WAIT." Blasted 23 push-ups in anti-feminist rage. Did 10, 7, 5, and 1.

Can't believe I'm delaying uni. I was making progress. Some girls had even started to use my first name.

TUE 24 FEB

Sister brought me back *Ultimate Bodybuilding* and smirked. I don't know why as the author, Mr Weider, is a trainer of champions. He discovered every training method and they all start with *Weider*. Even *weight* looks like *Weider*. He must like Arnold Schwarzenegger as he's everywhere. Arnold was ultimate by 19 so it won't take long.

Read about the *Weider Continuous Tension Principle* (sounds like my life), the *Weider Rest–Pause Principle* (sounds like my education), and the *Weider Overload Principle* (sounds like my mind). The last one's annoying as it says you must keep adding weight but I've got none to start with. Birthday's on Sunday so I'll put in a request.

WED 25 FEB

Every time you lift it's a *rep*. Every group of reps is a *set*. *Anabolic* means to build-up, *catabolic* to tear down. Mother's attitude is catabolic. There are big exercises where lots happens, *compound movements*. Then there's small ones where nothing happens, *isolation movements*. My life is now an isolation movement.

Mr Weider didn't name the muscles. The Latins did. Actually one muscle is Greek. The *deltoids* or shoulders. Sister has big shoulders. No wonder she won't cook.

Left my birthday list on the kitchen table. Wrote *Need weights*. Should have put *Need girls*.

THU 26 FEB

Mr Weider says it's important to check how you look as often as possible. Sister does it all the time. Dragged her big mirror into my room. I don't look like an ancient *Marvel* statue. I'm smaller and softer like a cherub. There are no cherubs in *Ultimate Bodybuilding*.

Sister came in room waving my birthday list and asked what it meant. How can she work in a library and not understand two words? I re-explained. She said I'm very changeable because I'm a Pisces. That's not true. At least I don't think it is? She shook her head and left. Then came back for her mirror.

FRI 27 FEB

Mr Weider says it's crucial to eat correctly. Most meals are chicken, broccoli and rice. Reminds me of school food and I squished that under my plate. He also talks about eating 6 times a day. Is that a printing error? He made no mention of my superfoods. I've used *Doritos Chilli Heatwave* and *Coke* to ace exams.

Think I did 30 push-ups today but on high numbers I lose count. It's all because mother never breast-fed me and damaged my brain. Feminists shouldn't have male babies if they abuse them.

SAT 28 FEB

Mother's coming here tomorrow to say hi but I know she's just collecting her stuff. If she was a proper parent she'd stay and let me resume my life. Birthdays taunt me with what I don't have.

At least my physical pains have gone. Only been doing it for two weeks and I'm already advanced. Still glad I'm getting weights tomorrow.

Mr Weider says measurements help track progress so I went into the bathroom with dad's tape. Changed my mind. Hadn't started on the muscles.

SUN 1 MAR

Happy birthday to me. If Bieber's born on the same day our mothers must have procreated on the same day. Why have I not procreated? If I don't procreate soon, I'll need a fake birth certificate.

9 a.m. No weights! Sister got me a used *Oxford English Dictionary*. Mother gave me weighing scales. I know they're the ones dad bought her, the ones she wouldn't stand on. Dad gave me an envelope with £42 inside (£2 for each year). On the back he wrote "Don't spend it on a woman."

10 a.m. Checked for birthday cards. Postal strike again. Mr Patel from next door left the *Bhagavad Gita* on our porch. His note said it's India's second-most famous book, and if I master it, I'll need their most famous.

4 p.m. Bought a big mirror. Snuck it into bedroom and stripped down to assess physique. Sister and mother burst in carrying cake. Mother said if that was my "birthday suit" I "better get a new one." Sister laughed so hard she blew out all my candles. The first two women to see me naked at 21 both laughed.

Got dressed and went for think-walk. Saw two girls smiling. They were smiling at another guy. Came back and thanked Mr Patel for the book. He said it's about overcoming fear. He asked "Are you a warrior, or are you a worrier?" I wasn't sure. He said not to worry.

Went home, jammed chair against my door, de-shirted. Checked the mirror to see if I resembled a warrior. Covered the mirror with *Finding Nemo* towel.

I'm annoyed to have a Sunday birthday but must stop letting the calendar bring me down. Starting today and every doomsday I'll find words that put the week in perspective.

SUNDAY SUM-UP

Failure is not an option.

- ARNOLD SCHWARZENEGGER

Weight: *140 lbs* (10 dictionaries)

MON 2 MAR

Bought 20 kilo dumbbell set from store. Got outside and the box split. Took a bus and the driver braked hard, discs everywhere. People stared as I picked them up. Some old guy said he used to lift weights but he looked like he couldn't lift a fork. Got off the bus, made weights into two 10 kilo dumbbells, and walked the rest. Met Mr Davenport going in. I said the dumbbells were part of my "birthday plan".

He got embarrassed about missing it, went into his garage, and came out with a weight bench. Said I could use it until Hugo gets back from uni. Known Hugo since 5 and can't believe he owns a bench. Hugo's doing a gap year, working. I'm doing a save-the-family year, and working out.

TUE 3 MAR

Can't shrug shoulders due to walking the weights home. According to Mr Weider the problem is my trapezius. The real problem is my trapezius isn't visible. Dad doesn't have it either. It is visible on sister and mother.

Finished *Ultimate Bodybuilding*. Know lots about Arnold now. His career started when Mr Weider bought him a plane ticket to America. Dad's worked in travel for years and never done that. And now he's fired. He looks amazing (Arnold, not dad). If I looked like him (Arnold, not dad) girls would never smile at another man.

WED 4 MAR

Properly started training. I'll do Mondays, Wednesdays and Fridays. Mr Weider calls it *full-body* even though my mind's not trained by it.

Dumbbell squats	2 x 15
Dumbbell row	2 x 10
Dumbbell bench press	2 x 10
Dumbbell flye	2 x 15
Dumbbell shoulder press	2 x 10 (only did one)
Dumbbell side raise	2 x 15
Dumbbell shrugs	2 x 10 (avoided)
Dumbbell lateral raise	2 x 10 (avoided)
Dumbbell overhead extension	2 x 10
Dumbbell curl	2 x 10
Dumbbell calf raise	1 x 20 (planned to do 2)
Crunches	1 x 20

Some need a barbell but I don't have one. Did calf raises on the stairs. Sister came out and said "Ballet boy." She will never get a boyfriend.

THU 5 MAR

Almost fell down the stairs! Body aches. The worst bit is under my arms and across my chest. Mr Weider says to make pain my friend. Surprised I've induced pain as I'm not sure if my technique's right. Some photos are unclear and that's despite no one having a shirt on. I can't risk training topless as feminists are vicious.

According to the dictionary, *muscle* comes from the word *mouse*. Instead of chicken, broccoli and rice, could I eat cheese?

FRI 6 MAR

Got a late gift from Hugo in the post, the *Tao Te Ching*. It's an old Chinese book like the self-help sister reads. Has that saying about the journey of a thousand miles beginning with the first step. Inside he wrote "Even wisdom's Made in China. See you in June."

Then got another book when sister came home. She plonked down *The Encyclopedia of Modern Bodybuilding* onto my lap. Bet she feels guilty about not cooking. It's written by Arnold and big like him. Couldn't stop looking at the photos. Everyone's shirtless again.

Got so inspired I did my workout twice. Now weigh less than ten dictionaries. Will use scales on alternate weeks to reduce negativity.

SAT 7 MAR

In Arnold's book there's a pic of an old strongman. He has an amazing physique but he's only wearing a leaf. A leaf to cover the rocket! *Calvin Klein* must be happy that look didn't catch on. Leaf man is *Eugene Sandow*. Mr Weider used Mr Sandow's body as the trophy for something called the *Mr Olympia*. If I won Mr Olympia I'd worry about grabbing Mr Sandow by the leaf.

SUN 8 MAR
INTERNATIONAL WOMEN'S DAY

Arnold says to train six days per week. I'd like to try it but I'm stiff at the moment. Suppose that's the price of progress. No progress in being stiff with females though. At uni, girls could see me, but here in the suburbs I'm a bluetooth device no longer discoverable. Need to turn bluetooth on and enhance pairing. Heard sister talking to friend about an app called *Tender*. Sounds like my ideal woman.

Today is *International Women's Day*. Women of the world, your wait for the perfect man is nearly over.

SUNDAY SUM-UP

The worst thing I can be is the same as everybody else.

- ARNOLD SCHWARZENEGGER

MON 9 MAR

Woke up in agony again. It's weird because I trained on Friday and felt fine at the weekend. I still did a workout today but everything felt painful to touch. Tender. Which reminds me I must look at that app and sign-up. Hopefully our internet can handle the traffic.

TUE 10 MAR

The app is not called *Tender* and nor are its females. Some ask for shirtless photos. What next, photos without a leaf? Anyway they can wait as I've found a problem. I look small in clothes but chubby out of them. The smallness is from dad and chub from mother. Must change so even Sherlock Holmes can't guess origins.

WED 11 MAR

Today's workout felt much stronger and the dumbbells didn't vibrate. On squats the weights were so light I did endless reps. But they're boring, burning, and I lose count. Should I get more weights? At this rate I'll need to lift mountains. In the meantime I'll listen to Arnold and train every day to make it harder.

I mean make *training* harder. The rocket works without training.

THU 12 MAR

Can't believe how expensive weight plates are. They're just blobs of metal and not designed by Steve Jobs. Could get used ones. Gravity works with objects of any age. Gravity makes dad's face sag.

FRI 13 MAR

Found a bargain on *eBay*. 50 kilos of plates for £20. The guy lives a mile away. I'll take my dumbbell handles, load them up, walk home. Collecting tomorrow. It might be Friday the 13th but the universe wants me to succeed. It says "Freddy Fox, you're no dumbbell."

SAT 14 MAR

Got to the guy's house and my dumbbells couldn't fit all the plates. He asked if I wanted a "long rod". Wasn't sure what he meant but he handed me a 5-foot barbell and said I could have it. Said he admired young men open to new things. If only my parents were this positive. He's a photographer and the weights were from a photoshoot. Gave me his business card. *Tom's Tripod.* Loaded up the barbell and walked home sideways. Got back looking like I was born with a spinal issue. Too tired to unload it so I did a light dumbbell workout. Also trained my shoulders using the Oxford Dictionary. I've named the exercise *Literal Raises.*

Now I've got a proper barbell, getting all the babes will be easy. The journey of a thousand girls begins with the first rep.

SUN 15 MAR
MOTHER'S DAY

Woke up feeling like my spine's been hit by a truck. Then realized I'd not bought a *Mother's Day* card. Then decided it should only apply to mothers who breast-fed.

Sister went out for her Sunday run so I stole her mirror to help see behind me. My back belongs to a woman in a movie and my calves are not born. Calves need mother's milk to grow. Returned sister's mirror and noticed her laptop on.

She had a *YouTube* video paused. I unpaused it for a sec. It was a muscular Chinese man called *Sick Abs Fast*. Him and another well-built guy were doing tug-of-war with a towel. No wonder she uses so many. I'd do it if I had someone to do it with. Couldn't do it with her as she's nuts and dad would topple.

SUNDAY SUM-UP

He who stands on tiptoe, doesn't stand firm.

- THE TAO TE CHING

Weight: 9.9 dictionaries

MON 16 MAR

Still feeling hit by truck. Decided to wait for pains to go and spent the day finishing Arnold's book. Can't ask her for another one so I'm wondering if I should go online? I suppose the online world still consists of words and I'll still have an advantage in translating those words. It's almost an unfair advantage. Right, that's it.

Won't ditch Arnie completely and will watch his documentary but refuse to let sister be the only Fox with big shoulders.

TUE 17 MAR
ST PATRICK'S DAY

So much info online. Started with forums. One site was called *bodybuilding.com* and full of wackos. People asked sensible questions but got bullied. The grammar errors were also scary. When it came to advice everyone said to drink milk and do deadlifts. I hate both. Can't acknowledge this place's bullying and blandness and will refer only to it as *the fiendish forum.* Felt overwhelmed so went for a think-walk. Saw drunks. Every St Patrick's Day everyone turns Irish. It's friendly but ethanol's still a drug. I'd never do drugs.

Came back and tried YouTube. The first two people I found were opposites. One calls himself *X-Man* and has none of mother's chubby genes. He's wiry with a Halloween face. Had endless videos but none wearing a shirt. X-Man used to help some baseball team. Must have been little league as he draws on himself with markers.

The next guy would scare kids. He's *Mitch Viola*, the most cartoonish human I've ever seen. And instead of using markers he's covered in actual dirty marks. I'd never get a tattoo. Tried to read his but they kept wobbling.

WED 18 MAR

Did barbell bench press for the first time. It's easier than dumbbells but also harder because I added more weight. Checked online for advice about bench pressing and found a guy called *The Other Jeff*. Who's the first one? This one's strong for a blond and has a great physique. He was also shirtless but that helped me learn technique. Once I did what he said the bench press felt better. So good I skipped my other exercises. I feel this movement does everything. Plus girls will mainly enjoy me from the front.

THU 19 MAR

Think I might be in love. Think I might love training. Focuses me like a book. Doing a rep stops me thinking about anything. Even uni. My only worry is that training might focus me too much. I trained today but I'm already thinking about training tomorrow. It's addictive because of the feeling I get after a set. The blood rush makes me feel brazen and the swelling is a glimpse into my future dimensions. Girls will soon glimpse my future swelling.

FRI 20 MAR

Almost died. I warmed-up on the bench press, felt good, and went to change weights. Pulled the plates off at the end nearest me and the barbell shot up my nose and between my eyebrows. Couldn't react.

Went to the mirror and peered around *Nemo*. My nose got grazed and there's a gash on my forehead. Mr Patel will assume I'm Hindu. Loving sister heard and shouted "Grow up."

Felt The Other Jeff didn't cover these dangers so found a "power-building" expert called *Sumo Fair*. He's not a sumo but he is bulky and shirtless. Felt depressed until he turned around and I saw his calves. They look like mine, walnuts in a hosepipe.

SAT 21 MAR

Went back to X-Man and Mitch Viola. The fitness world is diverse like a zoo. X-Man is cautious and warns what will "kill your gains". Don't have many to kill yet. Mitch Viola is gung-ho and looks like nothing could kill his gains or kill him. Is it because he eats so often? Heard him say 12 meals a day, i.e. double Mr Weider's approach. I'm still building up to three. Meals are stressful when there are no Fox females to make them.

SUN 22 MAR

Ate 3 times today (*Doritos* for lunch) and re-checked Mitch Viola's 12-meal theory. It's for special occasions. He drinks shakes but also suggests "real food". Are the shakes unreal? The fake-shakes could be handy as I can't get in the kitchen with sister's comfort gorging.

Looked for more food advice and found *Bate Body*. He drinks fizzy water and won't even eat until it's dark. How is he so big? Don't trust men who voluntarily drink fizzy water.

Watched *Pumping Iron*. Arnold's a slab of confidence. Felt sorry for Lou Ferrigno. His dad dominates like my mother and he said Arnold's arms were like spaghetti. Mine must be linguine. In one scene Arnold had girls on his back while he did "donkey calf raises". They were giggling at the donkey. I've never had two girls on my back. Or one. Arnold's a poet like me. He said the pump feels like the peak-moment with a woman. Cool metaphor. Cannot confirm.

SUNDAY SUM-UP

Milk is for babies.

- ARNOLD SCHWARZENEGGER

MON 23 MAR

Struggled to workout. Feel that Arnold's six days-a-week is for Austrians and the climate here is different. So I found an American called *Boston Barbell*. The English landed in Boston so his advice is more appropriate. He says I need rest days where I don't go near a "baaaahbell". He sounds like *Good Will Hunting* but with less math and more muscle. I'll do his suggestion, full-body three times a week, and not just bench press.

Boston Barbell also keeps his shirt off like X-Man. Does every American have a less critical mother than me?

TUE 24 MAR

Used today to rest and study diet. Find three meals hard but could try four. I can't tolerate the kitchen's female vibe. Plus if dad's not watching cartoons he wanders in and out like a zombie.

Watched a YouTuber called *Shaggy*. He had many food ideas and none required a woman. Things like peanut butter sandwiches and home-made protein drinks look okay. Everyone talks about protein.

Shaggy's chest is huge and he only bench presses on the floor. Did some and it felt good. Then did some on my bed. Might tell Mr Weider I've invented *Bed-Presses*.

WED 25 MAR

Today's workout was better. Arnold's advice almost terminated me. I've realized having a good workout comes down to how good each rep is. Each rep is a workout's smallest part, its atom. And today's reps were perfect. *Quality Atoms.*

At some point though I wanted to take my top off as sister was blasting the heating again. Didn't do it because de-shirting is a risk. Still recovering from childhood bath times. When I get my own place every door will have a lock.

Training covered does have one advantage. My clothes feel like they're about to burst their seams. I'll soon need to buy everything in medium.

THU 26 MAR

Before all this I ate whatever and whenever. Now I'm *trying* to eat. It's a pain but suppose it could be much worse. I could be a woman. They spend their days simultaneously loving and fearing the fridge.

At least resting is effortless. Different parts take longer to recover. Chest, triceps, biceps. Other bits of my anatomy always feel fine because they're always underused. Wrestling with the bald-headed champ never feels like a workout. Even if I do it twice on a Tuesday.

FRI 27 MAR

Been training a month and almost through all my weights. Feel I'm getting stronger more than I'm getting bigger. Went online to see what could be done without weights. Found *Mud Man*. He's a bald, black, bad ass. He spent years in jail and when guards took his weights he did bodyweight exercises. Even saw him use the Chinese towel technique. Considering how big he is I should be fine in my bedroom cell for a bit. He apparently ate lots of noodles though.

SAT 28 MAR

Tried noodles, felt ill. Mud Man must use special noodles. Searched for more diet ideas and for a moment thought Bieber had ballooned. Turns out to be a matching hedgehog called *Zeff Hyde*. His food advice was as wacky as his hair. Said eggs were for energy. To be sure I searched for "energy" and "eggs" and "muscle" and nothing came up. Actually there was one guy talking about "duck eggs". Will check that out later. Zeff reminds me of those silly guys, who silly girls like, yet the silly guys only love their silly selves. It's all very silly.

2 a.m. Wouldn't mind Zeff's outrageous physique. Or a silly girl.

SUN 29 MAR

My tops are getting tighter across the chest and shoulders but my sleeves feel baggy. What is wrong with my arms? I love training them but they're not loving me back. It could be my shoulders. My shoulders are starting to look good that my arms can't keep up.

That's like when simple people stand next to me and look simpler. I'll give myself until December to look amazing all over. Nine months is enough time to grow a baby. Including its new arms.

SUNDAY SUM-UP

The more you know, the less you understand.

- THE TAO TE CHING

Weight: *10.1 dictionaries*

MON 30 MAR

My arms are ruining my life. Ended up frustrated and cut today's workout short. Then cheered up by looking at idiots in gyms. A guy called *Mom's Spaghetti* is funny. At first I thought it was real advice because I used to do some of the stuff. But now a month in, and advanced, I can laugh at my old self.

TUE 31 MAR

Watched *Unbreakable* with Bruce Willis and Sam Jackson. Bruce has super genes and Sam hasn't so Sam wants what Bruce has. I'd never want what another man has. There's a bit where Bruce benches and keeps getting stronger. By the time the scene finishes he's run out of weights and realizes he's unbreakable. I'm running out of weights so maybe I'm unbreakable?

Mud Man keeps doing 10,000 calorie eating videos. It's called a "mukbang" in Korean and very popular. Do they really get excited by watching people pig-out? Might tip-off *Netflix* about their next easy market. I don't get it. Triggers thoughts of mother's enforced feeds.

2 a.m. Emailed Reed Hastings my ideas about Korean expansion.

WED 1 APR
APRIL FOOL'S DAY

Stupid film. Was feeling unbreakable doing bench press. Added weight slowly but couldn't calculate next increase so I put double on.

The first reps went okay. Then on rep four I touched my chest and it felt like I was pushing the ceiling. The only way the bar would move was forward. So I had to roll it. I rolled it over my chest (pain), over my stomach (more pain), and over my hip bones (massive pain). Just managed to wriggle out. Felt flattened by a steam roller and almost crushed the rocket before it's been used.

THU 2 APR

My accident wouldn't have happened if I'd been on a proper diet so in the absence of female chefs I ordered protein from *HustleTech*. Their site says I'll gain 15 pounds in a month. That's a dictionary plus 1 lb.

In all the protein-inspired excitement I found a YouTuber called *Compton Beef*. If thunder took human form he'd be it. And it seems I'm not the only one who forgets how many reps they've done. Every few minutes he reminds people it's *still* their "mother ****ing set." Find it hard to believe so many mothers do the ****ing but don't breast-feed the result.

FRI 3 APR
GOOD FRIDAY

Just read a disturbing survey in sister's *Vogue*. Girls voted men's arms the 3rd most attractive body part and I haven't got the first two. Some said they loved "grabbing" men's arms. It may be Good Friday but my arms are not grabbable so it's not good. I hope the *HustleTech* fixes it. Will all 15 pounds go to my arms? Wish it would arrive but no post on holidays. Jesus got crucified today then escaped from a sealed-up cave. I'd never escape with arms like these.

SAT 4 APR

According to Mitch Viola, the key to bigger arms is to train them with 8-hour workouts. If I sleep for 8 hours, and am awake for 16, isn't half my existence training? The maths is troubling. But it's also exciting. His video title said I can ADD 1" INCH IN ONE DAY. Originally clicked on it for other reasons.

SUN 5 APR
EASTER SUNDAY

So quiet I wrote a Japanese "haiku" about my bench press incident.

Pressed and up lifted
Kilos high and next no air
Weight of rock drops south

First Easter Sunday without Mother. She always gave me an egg. Also known as a bovine-based bribe for not breast-feeding me.

2 a.m. No reply from Reed Hastings yet. Maybe he's forgotten? Maybe he wasn't breast-fed? I can tell Bezos was.

SUNDAY SUM-UP

Ordinary men hate solitude, but the master makes use of it.

- THE TAO TE CHING

MON 6 APR
INTERNATIONAL DNA DAY

8 a.m.	Big breakfast! About to do Viola's 8-hour arms!
9 a.m.	*HustleTech* arrived! Thanks Universe!
10 a.m.	First workout! Sets, sets, sets! I'm a sets addict!
11 a.m.	Second workout! Shake gritty! Viola's a genius!
12 p.m.	Third! Arms look like someone else's! Look grabbable!
1 p.m.	Fourth. Arms not more grabbable in last hour.
2 p.m.	Fifth. Arms hurting. Looking like mine again.
3 p.m.	Sixth. Spine shattered. I am breakable.
4 p.m.	Seventh. Did Viola get this wrong?

5 p.m.   Eighth. If only girls knew the pains of man.
6 p.m.   Done 40 sets of biceps, 40 triceps. Never again.
7 p.m.   Had shakes every two hours and extra one now.
8 p.m.   Stomach gurgling non-stop and full of air.

On bed. Couldn't do last shake as arms too weak to shake shaker. Today's when two scientists presented DNA to the world and they won a *Nobel*. Doubt I'd give either Fox parent a prize for my particular double helix. Think genes are like floors of a building. Some people are at the bottom, some are in the middle, and some are at the top. My shoulders have penthouse genetics but my arms are basement. Today should bring them up to first-floor.

12 a.m.   Toilet.
1 a.m.   Toilet.
2 a.m.   Toilet. Stupid *HustleTech*.

TUE 7 APR

Against animal testing and now hate human experiments. My right arm measures only ½ an inch bigger and can't flex the left. Either way they still sound small. Will date a European girl as they use metric and arms sound better in centimetres. Everything does.

WED 8 APR

Immense soreness. Couldn't train as arms and spine hurt even in non-arm movements. Watched *Rocky* for inspiration. In one scene he drank 5 eggs before training. Were they duck eggs? Will look up.

Arms only ¼" (6 mm) bigger now. What if I've damaged them and they keep shrinking? Can't get girls if my arms look like theirs.

THU 9 APR

Right arm now the same size as before. Left arm smaller. Might be from wrestling the bald-headed champ to elevate my lowered mood. Rocky avoided it before fights as it saps strength. Have to respect such discipline especially as someone would wrestle for him.

Found the man who sells anabolic eggs, *Dirk O' Flynn*. He must be using them because he's solid and strong. Even his face is like tough plastic, a human *Ken* doll on steroids. But I know he doesn't do drugs as he says so. Saw a video where he posed next to Mitch Viola, who does use drugs, making Dirk extra impressive for using nature. They were hanging out at the swanky *Gold's Gym Venice*, California. Dirk must be partially-sighted because he squints at the mirror and is followed around by a dog.

FRI 10 APR

Dirk O' Flynn won't ship duck eggs here! You flaunt a secret but refuse to share? Some men are so competitive and that's because they're insecure. If I had duck eggs and trained in a top gym I'd give Dirk a run for his money.

Dad left his wedding album open on the kitchen table. Today's their anniversary. They wanted to get married on Valentine's but it was fully-booked so they got April 10. That's when *Titanic* set sail. He's slim in the pics but mother isn't. Read *Ultimate Bodybuilding* to see what Mr Weider said about genetics. Had to stop. Got upsetting.

SAT 11 APR

Think the problem with *HustleTech* is that I mixed it with milk and I hate milk. Every time I drink it my stomach makes rubber band noises. Sister says I'm "lactose intolerant". I'm intolerant to her amateur doctoring. Looked for alternatives and they're never ending. Who can I trust in such a situation? Not sister. Women like her love blocking male progress. Gets it from mother. Both were breast-fed.

SUN 12 APR

Went back to The Other Jeff as he had diet videos and male blonds don't lie. In one he spoke to an expert called *Chad Showcracker PhD*. He knows everything about "hypertrophy", the science of muscle growth i.e. getting girls. According to Chad, I need 100 grams of protein per day. That's 10 grams *per dictionary* of bodyweight. Not sure I should trust him. He's dad's age but wears a baseball cap. Anyone with a baseball cap and mortgage at the same time is crazy.

2 a.m. Dr Google says I'm lactose intolerant. Won't tell sister.

SUNDAY SUM-UP

He who eats too much, or too little, will never succeed.

- THE BHAGAVAD GITA

Weight: *10.2 dictionaries*

MON 13 APR

Waited until sister left for work then went in the kitchen and found food scales. *HustleTech* scoop is faulty. Says it measures 30 grams of powder but it's 20. I've been using one scoop apart from the first day when I got excited and did double. If I use it more I'll get through a tub in a week. These people are drug dealers.

Did workout but saved protein powder for dinner. According to Chad Showcracker PhD, I don't need it after training as long as I get enough in total.

Now sister has assumed the mother role I'll demand she buys more food protein. Otherwise she'll be the second Fox female to commit nutrient abuse.

TUE 14 APR

Showcracker is crackers! Did exactly what he said and got enough protein in total but didn't have any after training. Woke up feeling way more sore. That's the last time I listen to anyone my size.

Found out the *HustleTech* is "whey" protein and whey comes from cheese and cheese is milk's in-bred cousin and milk is breast-food for baby cows. I won't deprive them like mother did to me. Will finish what I have then ban anything to do with breast-feeding. But won't ban the breast.

WED 15 APR

Did my workout and went to make an anti-Chad shake immediately. Did it so fast I didn't do the lid. Saw drips on the walls and had to clean it up like a crime scene. If sister saw the evidence she'd love it.

She's gagging to tell me I should eat "real food". Does that mean she's been watching Mitch Viola?

THU 16 APR

Feel more recovered today and I know it's because I had a shake after yesterday's workout. Googled around and the eating time right after a workout is called the *anabolic window*. People call that "broscience" which is slang for gym knowledge that's now inaccurate. I say people have forgotten the slang "No smoke without fire." If the common man sees smoke and feels he can put out the fire with a shake after training, why not? I don't trust geeks now. Actually I've never trusted professions that wear white.

Broscience isn't that bad but think I'll trust ownscience.

FRI 17 APR

Sister came home way too early and caught me mid-training. Thought I'd got away without a comment but as I swung the door she laughed and said "Body dysmorphia." That was all she said. Obviously she picked it up from *Vogue*. Body dysmorphia! These journalists love making up words. And if she thinks I'll take the bait she thinks wrong. Nothing will stop me becoming perfect.

SAT 18 APR

My physique is lopsided, almost bordering on deformity. Now it will be especially hard to look in the mirror. Went back to Mr Weider. He said symmetry's very important. Thought he meant just for people in bodybuilding shows. I'd never be in bodybuilding shows. Then remembered the book on ancients and even sculptors made their statues balanced. They didn't give them one bicep bigger or one pec major majorly higher. And when it comes to pecs theirs were straight across the bottom. Mine are more curved. Dad's chest belongs to a malnourished woman from the third world.

2 a.m. Woke up worried about chest. Was scared to look but had to confirm fears. They were confirmed. My chest still looks wonky in the moonlight.

SUN 19 APR
1962 - DORIAN YATES BORN

Watched old clips of Arnold having fun in Venice Beach. Bet there's no Sunday feeling in Venice. After watching Arnold I kept seeing ads for a fitness expo coming here. Could it be my chance to taste the Venice lifestyle, my chance to meet tasty girls?

Mitch Viola was in the ad but also names I didn't know including a minor British champion called Dorian Yates. Must be named after Oscar Wilde's *The Picture of Dorian Gray*. Mr Gray gets his painting done then but worries about how he'll look in comparison as he ages. So he sells his soul in exchange for never aging. One day he actually gets fed up looking great and slashes the painting. His servants hear a crash and discover him dead by the exact same slashes.

I do worry about looking older because people will expect me to know about older pleasures. Bet the expo could fix that. And with all the Americans coming over, I bet Dorian could do with my support.

SUNDAY SUM-UP

Only shallow people do not judge by appearances.

- A PICTURE OF DORIAN GRAY BY OSCAR WILDE

MON 20 APR

Felt strong today which I assume is the weekend rest. Went for a think-walk and stopped by the electrical store. I assessed myself on-camera and a member of staff peered through the window again. The universe is training me to be stared at. I look pretty good with two sweatshirts. They say the camera adds 10 pounds even though my scales don't show that. It's lucky girls don't weigh guys.

Came home excited and looked up the fitness expo. It's called *Bodypower*. Feels like they named it after me.

TUE 21 APR

Watched *Rocky 4*. For a film that's old as dad it was good. The story is a big fight between America and Russia. America, through Rocky Balboa, trains using hard work and nature.

And Russia, through Ivan Drago, uses drugs and technology. Of course the USA wins. Despite Rocky's old school approach he didn't drink eggs in this one. Bet he moved on to *HustleTech*.

WED 22 APR

Discovered the *Dodge Twins*. They're identically big but their personalities are unidentical. Marvin is bonkers while Mike's the straight-man. Both shout and get close to the camera. They've got big backs and legs yet neither deadlifts or squats because of an injury they incurred in *Snap City*. Couldn't find it on *Wikipedia*.

My back's been dodgy since I walked that loaded barbell home. They do a squat alternative which I'll try especially as I don't want to end up with dad's posture. From the side he looks like a question mark.

Handy to be an identical twin. Although you couldn't lie about your measurements. Any of them.

THU 23 APR

Looked up *Rocky 4*. In 1983 Russia was drugging their athletes to dominate the L.A. Olympics. Stallone wanted to tell the world and make America look squeaky clean. But they weren't squeaky clean. They were slow. Russia started using steroids in 1954.

That year, at a weightlifting event, the Russian and American coaches got drunk after dinner. The American asked the Russian what his winning secret was and he told him. The American rushed home, and by 1958, US scientists had invented their own steroids. The American coaches then dished them out like candy and soon started winning. That'll teach the Russians to hold their vodka.

Still wouldn't mess with Russia. Saw a clip of President Putin riding a horse while shirtless. Can't see Boris Johnson doing that. The horse would need steroids just to stop it being crushed.

FRI 24 APR

Empty house as sister at work and dad on cartoons. Realized I train calmer in peace and that slower reps lead to faster swelling. Used to rush in the beginning when the weights looked light.

But that was my training childhood and I won't let it ruin my training adulthood. One of sister's self-help books said we should dance like no one's watching. I must train like she's not watching.

Tried out the "goblet" squat mentioned by the Dodge Twins. They must like *Harry Potter*. The weight was girly but it made my legs feel manly. Then watched more Dodge Twins as I downed my anti-Chad. The twins end every one of their videos saying I can do "whatever the ****" I want. So I did. I booked Bodypower.

There will be no identical twin of me there. No sir, I'm a one-off.

SAT 25 APR

So many Americans coming to Bodypower. They'll be shocked by the lack of beaches and beach bodies in Birmingham.
I must fly the flag and show them we don't all look like blobs. And it will be good for me as sister's books say positive feedback boosts motivation.

Found a vest I can wear. It's a junior school PE vest but it still fits. I could almost be the new Bruce Lee. What if people stop me and ask for photos? Better practice smiling.

SUN 26 APR

London Marathon today. Watched it on TV as I ate breakfast and they burned theirs. Then caught a glimpse of myself brushing my teeth. Thought I looked like a moderately big marathon runner. While that's good enough for Bruce Lee it's not good enough for me. Might have to consult Mr Weider's writings about aerobic exercise. Due to my intellect, I'm always walking, and due to other guy's lack of intellect, I'm sometimes running.

SUNDAY SUM-UP

I'm not in this world to live up to your expectations,
And you're not in this world to live up to mine.

- BRUCE LEE

Weight: *10.3 dictionaries*

MON 27 APR

She's actually done it. Mother's divorcing dad and the papers landed on the doormat. I can tell that's what they are because dad stared at the envelope but wouldn't pick it up. What kind of man has a fear of envelopes? Envelopes contain words and words are joy. When the man of the house came home she picked it up immediately. Told sister it was none of her business. She said her business was harmony.

When girls approach at Bodypower I'll tell the story of my broken home. According to science, sympathy is a powerful aphrodisiac.

TUE 28 APR

On the days between workouts, I'm smaller. Did research and everyone claims rest days are when you grow so I must double my kitchen visits. They say eating carbs fills-up muscles like a sponge. That means if I don't eat enough the sponges will look wrung-out and not grow. My arms look wrung-out.

Searched YouTube for arm advice and found a channel called *More Curls, More Girls*. I bet the guy who runs it, Kreed, read the *Vogue* survey. Didn't see any arm videos though. He highlights the importance of good hair and good hormones. Think I have 50% of those. Kreed reminds me of me. He's upbeat, but with concerned eyes, the eyes of a sensitive soul who carries some deep past on his shoulders. His shoulders do not remind me of me.

WED 29 APR

Filled up the sponges by eating much more and my arms look better. Now I've found another problem. The *brachialis* muscle. According to the dictionary it means "belonging to the arm" and it belongs to my arm. Supposed to be a visible bulge on the outside but my bulge is invisible.

Why is mine missing? Did it dissolve in the womb? Surely doctors would have noticed at my birth? Or has a lack of breast-feeding stunted it? Would have thought the 8-hour arm workout did something. Arms are crucial. They're the only semi-exposed part of my body until I reveal more. Brachialis, come out, come out, wherever you are.

THU 30 APR

Got six scoops of *HustleTech* left but thoughts of mother stunting my brachialis mean I can't face it. Will put it aside for emergencies. Going to try those Shaggy snacks, the peanut butter stuff. Might do wholemeal bread for the protein even though I hate wholemeal. It's one of those adult tastes like coffee or cous-cous or watching CNN.

FRI 1 MAY

Didn't train until I demolished a whole loaf with peanut butter. Sister decided she was a chef after all, and when she went to make a sandwich, saw the bread deficit and went bonkers. Told her it was dad's divorce eating and she stormed off.

Got such a good pump today, felt brazen from the bread. Reminded me about Arnold's "peak-moment" metaphor so I booked my hotel for Bodypower. Paid for Friday and Saturday, check-out Sunday. That's plenty of time for me to check-out a Venice Beach babe. I'm even prepared to offer my innocence to a British girl. Ordered a "superior" room with king size bed. All I need now is a superior princess.

SAT 2 MAY

The loaf with peanut butter made my stomach ping all night. Researched alternatives. Came down to beef protein or plant protein. I used to enjoy a steak but the thought of crushed cow made me gag. Even Rocky wouldn't do that.

Wasn't sure about plant stuff so looked into it. Found a channel called *Veggie 'Sults*. Not sure if *'Sults* means *results* or *insults* because the guy had big arms but was also vicious. But he wasn't wearing white so I ordered some plants and hopefully won't become a rabbit.

Can't believe I'm going to eat vegetables. Will girls even realize my efforts to enrich their lives?

2 a.m. Apparently rabbits are one of the most sexually successful species. It's why *Playboy Bunnies* are bunnies.

SUN 3 MAY

Searched for info about the brachialis. Everyone said the same thing, that it works whenever you do biceps. Chad Showcracker PhD could have told me that! Useless.

Went back to X-Man and he was worse. His whole thing is to dismiss everything that kills gains. If I wanted such a cavalier attitude I'd ask sister. Then did an image search for the brachialis and even some professional bodybuilders don't have it.

Feel relieved knowing it's just one of those things. And the main thing is no girl mentioned it in the *Vogue* survey.

SUNDAY SUM-UP

You either got it, or you don't got it.

- DORIAN YATES

MON 4 MAY
MAY BANK HOLIDAY

Holidays depress me. The office slaves are at home, mowing lawns, drilling, or fixing anything but themselves. Dad made it more depressing by opening the divorce papers.

Only did a light workout while I wait for the new protein. Decided to boost my nutrition know-how in the meantime and found a British version of Chad Showcracker PhD. The channel's called *Menial Jerks*. He hates people in the fitness industry which explains the name. He says people take drugs but pretend they don't. If that's true they are menial jerks. Dirk O' Flynn is a menial jerk for pretending he'll ship duck eggs here.

TUE 5 MAY

Watched more Menial Jerks. He has endless videos on "fake nattys". They are fake naturals, people who take the Ivan Drago drug road but claim clean as Rocky. Couldn't understand why anyone would lie but MJ says it's about money. Fake nattys get trainees to buy supplements or programs by promising it will make them *Marvel*. Had a quick look around and he could be right.

There was a guy called *Saint Vince* who's not a saint because when he speaks he doesn't believe what he's preaching. He's obviously a front-man who's being used for his looks. Obviously I wouldn't mind being used for my looks. Lucky Mr Weider tutored me, but I still object to him being a front-man for chicken, broccoli and rice.

2 a.m. Looked up *natty* because it means something different here. According to the dictionary, it's from *neat* and means well-dressed. In Mr Weider's book and Arnold's book no one had clothes on. Therefore in the British sense, they can't be natty.

WED 6 MAY
1954 - BRITISH ATHLETE ROGER BANNISTER BREAKS THE 4-MINUTE MILE

Lost my patience with high-rep squats. Can't fit more weight onto the goblet version so I'll skip legs for now. What's the point in diverting energy to parts girls won't see? And I won't train calves. Calves didn't even make the *Vogue* top ten. Plus every time I use them sister insults me. They help running but I don't run since Mr Weider confirmed it can cause shrinkage. Today's when Roger Bannister's running broke the 4-minute mile. I can do equally exciting things in under 4 minutes but no one gives me a medal.

THU 7 MAY

Much better to skip legs. Realize that tiredness comes from how they feel. When they're dull I don't feel like doing anything and I have way more spring in my step today. I reckon people who train legs all the time are depressed all the time. The opposite isn't true though. Dad does zero training and he's depressed non-stop.

The rabbit food I ordered is called *Quad Power* even though it has nothing to do with legs and is animal leg-free. "Quad" means four proteins: *peas*, *hemp*, *soy* and *rice*. I'm annoyed that rice has snuck into my diet, but as long as I don't taste it, it doesn't exist.

FRI 8 MAY

This time next week I'll get to show my other side. Who else can shift from Shakespeare to shoulders in an instant? If Shakespeare had my shoulders he'd write about them.

Protein, protein, where art thou protein? There's no post on Sundays which means unless it arrives tomorrow I'll only have a few days to use it pre-expo. And for the ladies, that would be a tragedy.

SAT 9 MAY

Got up for breakfast and found dad scribbling notes on the kitchen table. He wrote "Grounds for divorce" at the top and underneath had crossed-out: *adultery, violence, drink, not paying way, desertion*. Wasn't the greatest start to the day but then the doorbell chimed and we both went. It was all the rabbit food and my Bodypower ticket. Dad smiled at the delivery guy and said "You see, there's nothing she can do." Delivery guy hurried away. Will try the protein when it's quiet as sister's off work and ready to pounce.

SUN 10 MAY

Watched *Generation Iron* documentary to soothe away Sunday blues. Think they wanted it to be a modern *Pumping Iron*. The physiques were bigger but the personalities had shrunk. There was an exception called Kai Greene. He's also a poet although he seemed to speak another language at times. Mr Greene has an impressive physique but he's not touched Mr Sandow's leaf. I think he could but the show organizers might fear his victory speech. His rival is Phil Heath. He's touched Mr Sandow many times and it's made him cocky. I'm not sure Kai's made to be a bodybuilder. When a sensitive soul has to keep fighting a tough opponent the battles start to hurt. I've learned this repeatedly facing mother.

Sister went for her run so I tried the *Quad Power*. Stomach pinged louder than ever! If I meet a girl I can't have protein close to the time, but if I've had a workout, I must have protein. So I can't mix girls and workouts? Modern relationships are complicated.

SUNDAY SUM-UP

If you micro-manage your life it's a very uncomfortable way of living.

- KAI GREENE

Weight: *10.3 dictionaries*

MON 11 MAY

Had *Quad Power* at breakfast and the pinging sounds were gone. Also tastes fine without bovine breast-milk.

Getting fascinated with the fitness subculture in the build-up to Bodypower. It's chock-full of freaks, psychos, saddos, and scandal. Won't be long 'til TMZ realizes the potential. In the meantime I found a channel called *The Kentucky Kid* who covers it.

Not being gay, but he has a soothing voice that makes the wacky stories seem wackier. Hope the channel isn't propaganda for fried chicken. Or broccoli. Or rice.

TUE 12 MAY

Went back to Menial Jerks to get his thoughts on protein. As with all intellects he gave vague answers. It's a truth of life that only the shady are certain. He also hinted that Dirk O' Flynn was shady and doesn't rely on nature. That's disappointing but at least it explains his face. It's so taut I couldn't read his body language.

Menial had a playlist on supplements. Dirk's duck eggs were absent but he mentioned *creatine monohydrate*. It's an energy molecule, and even though the body makes it, the factory-made version is better. Every shirtless YouTuber takes it so I ordered some from Jeff's Jumble.

Menial Jerks is never shirtless and that's a British thing. I might be the only Brit in a vest at Bodypower. But if I meet the lucky girl, she could lie back and watch me finish the day vest-free.

WED 13 MAY

Jeff's Jumble delivered the creatine. Bet Bezos built *Prime* on it. Doesn't taste like it's from a factory. Tastes like sand so maybe that's why it builds a beach body. Label says to do 20 grams a day for the first 5 days. That means a third of my tub will be gone in a week. Mind you it's a crucial week and I can't be underpowered at Bodypower. Will do 3 scoops before bed to make sure people notice my factory-made enhancements.

It's weird how no one from here ever built a body. We just grow potatoes, eat them, and become them.

2 a.m. Stomach in agony and it's not the rabbit food. Looked up creatine and even Chad Showcracker PhD said the "loading" phase wasn't needed. Said it was "broscience" and could upset the stomach. Will take one scoop a day from daylight. Assuming I wake up.

THU 14 MAY
ASCENSION DAY

Sister's running a library discussion group for those affected by "unrealistic online influences". Reckons men will attend. Not me. Don't people realize they're looking at a skewed distribution? The only good physiques are Californian so there really aren't that many.
If an alien landed in an ice cream parlour they'd assume all human food was ice cream when it's not. The fitness industry's just a little ice cream parlour.

Creatine hasn't made me different yet, and during my test of the vest, I couldn't see a brachialis. I look good though, and if I hold my lamp at a certain angle and my breath, I almost look menacing. Might even look like I'm from the Californian ice cream parlour.

Today's *Ascension Day*, the day when Jesus floated up to heaven. But today can wait because it's all about tomorrow. Tomorrow's my time to ascend. Tomorrow, Freddy Fox will find female disciples.

FRI 15 MAY

9 a.m.   On train to Birmingham, Bodypower, babes!
10   People getting on wearing brightly-colored clothes.
10.30   Brightly-colored clothing people constantly eating.
12 p.m.   Outside expo in line, people tanned without sun.
12.05   Took off hoodie and put it around waist.
12.10   Inside. It's a bodybuilding *IKEA*. Lost hoodie.
12.15   Feeling a bit exposed in my white vest.
12.20   Saw Mitch Viola's booth *2% FOR LIFE*. Promoting milk?
12.25   Endless YouTuber types but don't know names.
12.30   Big stage area with Bieber-boys dancing on it, arms twirling above heads. A gay porn set?
12.35   Gay porn set is a clothing company called *Fit-Fish*.
12.40   Hit by two porn set t-shirts. Gave one to boy next to me who sprayed his shorts with joy.

1	Lots of booths with pretty girls working at them. Failed to get their attention. Non-binary? Business-obsessed? Non-binary and business-obsessed?
2	Think people are staring at my vest.
2.15	Saw Dodge Twins from *Snap City, USA.*
2.30	No girls looking. Am I that intimidating?
3	Put Fit-Fish t-shirt on in toilets. Label says XL but it fits like a child's wet-suit.
3.30	We're no longer a nation of potatoes. We're pineapples or some other muscular plant.
4.05	Quit expo. Sitting in pasta place, dressed in scuba gear.
6 p.m.	Checked-in at hotel. On bed. Why are so many people are into training? They can't all have a year off from uni. And why do so many have big arms? Better not live near me.

SAT 16 MAY

9 a.m.	Hotel dining room. Bodybuilders destroying all-you-can-eat breakfast. Manager in tears.
10	Outside expo in longer line than yesterday.
11	Inside at last. Packed *IKEA* again. Bit panicky again.
12 p.m.	Saw *Catford Koala* and *Odysseus*. YouTubers? Mitch Viola 2% milk stand busier. Fit-Fish stage males being female.
1	Every girl has a backside like a bumper car.
1.30	Am I the smallest one here?
3.30	Sat against expo walls behind the booths. Couldn't take being shoved around and drowned by a river of muscle. Been here ages. Will do one last circuit or it's a wasted trip.
4	Stumbled on *DY Nutrition*. All the staff friendly. They're doing a seminar tomorrow at a local gym so I got a ticket. Blown my money but it's better than coming back here. Plus got a hoodie and book as part of the deal. Powerful looking guy at the back of their booth gave me a nod. It's not female attention, but still.
6 p.m.	In hotel room alone and single but eating family-sized pizza. The training book is *A Portrait of Dorian Yates.* Think he's the guy who nodded at me and the minor British champion I saw on the ad. He's taking tomorrow's seminar. Not sure he needs my help fending-off the Americans.

11 p.m.   Should have looked up previous Bodypower footage before. Then I wouldn't have been exposed in an ice cream parlour. What a Fox-up.

SUN 17 MAY

10 a.m.   Outside a place called *Temple Gym*. Is it religion and training combined? Starts in 15. A few have gone in.

10.05   Everyone's in now. Put on "DY" hoodie for confidence. Parachute. Looks like I've shrunk. Confidence also shrunk.

10.10   A woman went in! Like a muscular gypsy. We both stared.

10.30   Back at hotel. I got half way down the stairs and it sounded like Churchill commanding troops from his bunker. Freaked out. Retreated. Lost the war on muscle. What's wrong with me? Leaving Fit-Fish shirt. Might fit a maid.

9 p.m.   In bedroom at Fox-hole. No girls noticed me. That is feedback but not the kind I wanted.

10 p.m.   Will I only ever screw dumbbell collars?

11 p.m.   Is mother right, am I not made for this? If genes are an act of god she should give me my money back.

2 a.m.   I still like training, just not sure I like myself. Today's been a Five-Star Fox-Up. I hate Sundays.

SUNDAY SUM-UP

There's only one thing worse than being talked about,
And that is not being talked about.

- A PICTURE OF DORIAN GRAY BY OSCAR WILDE

Weight: *Tiny*

MON 18 MAY

Woke up feeling especially dumb this morning. Didn't know where to turn so I went to the place that has never failed me. Words. Started reading *A Portrait of Dorian Yates*. The opening section's called "What Makes Dorian Run?" It's about him jogging at school during some sports day. After 15 laps, everyone quit. Dorian, unlike them and unlike me, didn't quit. At lap 45 he was still going strong and the teachers begged him to stop. *What Makes Freddy Run?* 50,000 guys at an expo. All with bigger arms.

TUE 19 MAY

I know exactly why my body's out of date. *Ultimate Bodybuilding* is out of date. So is Arnie's book. But Dorian's is recent and he's not actually a minor champion. He's touched Mr Sandow's leaf six times. Unlike Arnold, he suggests spending less time training, but doing it with more manliness. This appeals to me. My legs never got bigger from the 1000 reps called walking. And our postman walks reps non-stop but still resembles a giraffe.

2 a.m. Mr Yates has challenged my theory about blond men.

WED 20 MAY

Went into my bedroom and found sister doing squats. With my weights, by my mirror, *Nemo* flung on the floor. She calmly finished a set of 20 then turned and said "Thought you weren't using them." Not using them? Not using them? When was I not using them? Not using them that day? Or not using them ever? How dare she.

No girls showed me respect at the expo either. No girls noticed. Girls have never noticed me, at least not first. They always look at other guys first. I'm always the clown watching guys get looked at.

That's it. I won't be bullied by Bodypower, blind babes, and sister in the same week. I must accept that females have a limited capacity for knowing who I am based on my exterior. And I must overcome their disability by changing my exterior. I must change it massively. But not here. It's time to go public.

Will gather up my weights and put them right outside her door. Enjoy your trip! Put *Nemo* back over mirror. Only a girl would disrespect a man's towel.

THU 21 MAY

Spent all day looking for local gyms. Made a shortlist:

Royal & Racket
The Iron Pit
Sparkles

Doubt it makes a difference as long as sister's not there. Continued reading Dorian's book. He says it's best to do a warm-up then one or two all-out sets. He says once you've hit a muscle, extra sets make it harder to recover. I like his gangster metaphor about not bothering to hit a man who's already down. If only mother understood this during my childhood.

FRI 22 MAY

Went to *Royal & Racket*. It's a posh tennis club. Told the posh lady I was interested in the gym but she showed me everything else. She asked who my favorite tennis player was, so I said "Nadal", hoping his muscularity would get her to show me the gym. She continued with the squash courts, snooker table, and bar. Finally, her brain clicked and she said "Oh yes, the gymmy gym." The gymmy gym was a tiny room, with tiny dumbbells, and a few old machines. If Nadal trained here, he'd be tiny.

SAT 23 MAY

Phoned *Sparkles* and they said to just come down. Showed up and then told to make an appointment. People who work with the public have the highest level of retardation. I'd never work with the public. Going again on Monday. While I was there, I saw lots of equipment, and lots of girls. Strangely, more girls than guys. I don't mind though. Nor will they. They'll soon be staring at my equipment.

SUN 24 MAY

Phoned *The Iron Pit* but no one picked-up. Sister went out for her long run so I snuck into her room to use my weights. Put everything back, snuck back out, had anti-Chad and continued Dorian's book.

    He says it's good to train a muscle less often. Twice a week max. He calls it "high-intensity training". Says he explains it all in his documentary, *Blood & Guts*. When I left Birmingham I had no guts.

SUNDAY SUM-UP

You want to be really outstanding?
You've just got to forget about normal life.

- DORIAN YATES

MON 25 MAY
SPRING BANK HOLIDAY

Went to *Sparkles* and sat around for ages. Laughed at their slogan *WHERE WELLNESS NEVER SLEEPS*. They might be open 24 hours but "wellness" isn't a word at any time. Eventually the sales manager showed up and made me fill in two forms. Two forms to look around! It's not the *Pentagon*. One form was about goals.

What areas would you like our help with?

Weight loss   ☐
Toning   ☐
Rehab   ☐
Fitness   ☐
Body-building ☐
Social   ☐

Didn't tick *body-building* because it was embarrassing and incorrectly hyphenated. What the hell is "Social"? Ticked *Fitness* and *Rehab* even though I'm fit as a horse and will never need rehab. Sales manager nodded at the form then we wandered. Showed me the changing rooms, showers, sauna, and the aerobics studio. *Zumba* was on and I saw rows of bouncing buttocks.

As we walked around I wondered why people always show me non-gym stuff first? When we did go into the gym it had loads of machines, pulley things, barbells, and loads of dumbbells. I wanted to try the heaviest but his lingering put me off. He explained the simple membership, which was complicated, then we shook hands and I left. Didn't take in all the details and he didn't take in whose hand he shook. The hand of a man on a mission.

TUE 26 MAY

Phoned *The Iron Pit* again and still no one picked-up. Bet it's out of business. *Sparkles* is fine. It's a bit pink and a bit corporate but I must do something a bit soon.

Watched *The Wrestler*. The actor Mickey Rourke plays a washed-up, once-famous wrestler who has broken relationships with most of his family. I related to his pain and could confirm its realism. What's more impressive is how he played a man full of steroids by pretending. These guys are worth their paychecks. I'll consider being a movie star if the poetry doesn't work out. Bit unsure about being shirtless though. Matthew McConaughey only does shirtless movies so I'd do the covered-up roles he'd struggle with.

WED 27 MAY

Mrs Fox called out of the blue and disturbed me deeply. My mother, my birth vessel, has met a man. Awful. And he has an awful name. *Sinclair*. In one call I realized my mother knows nothing about her son. She said he's my kind of guy, she said he had a great body, and she said we should all meet up. Told her I'd think about meeting which is Freddy-speak for not-a-chance. The only thing I did agree with was calling him "Sin". Ten minutes later she texted his photo and said "What do you think?" I didn't reply. Relieved it was just his face. Then the other Fox female asked me if I had "any more weights?" What the Fox? Must choose a gym urgently. And not let her follow.

THU 28 MAY

Gave *The Iron Pit* one final chance and called again. They never answer and they haven't even got a website.

Had a look for other places but they're all too far. Something near is best as I prefer to shower privates in private. That's not even possible at home as the bathroom door is still lockless.

According to *Vogue*, Mr McConaughey is only the *third* most shirtless actor in Hollywood. Stallone is *second* and Daniel Craig *first*. Sly's played *Rocky* 6 times and *Rambo* 5 times. How does Craig beat that? He must be a show-off Leo like Mr McConaughey or dad. They need no excuse to laze around like vain naked lions.

2 a.m. Daniel Craig is born a day after me. His Piscean imagination has gone to his head. Must be the false confidence of him being *007*. I could do that. The name's Fox, Freddy Fox...

FRI 29 MAY

Woke up after a *Spectator ONLY* dream and decided it was an omen. Called *Sparkles* and joined over the phone. They said I "need" an induction. Why must I be induced? I own three books on training, two big dictionaries, and a 170 IQ. Einstein maxed out at just 160. He would need an induction.

SAT 30 MAY

Read something odd in *A Portrait of Dorian Yates*. He says the change from intermediate to advanced should "not be dramatic". Think that means I should keep a low profile at the gym. I'll wear grey. Rocky wears grey. What's also odd are Dorian's muscles. Compared to those in Mr Weider's book and Arnold's, his muscles are statue-like. Like stone. Like grey granite. Even compared to the Californians his body seems different. Some people are big, and some people are granite-looking, but he's both. I'm currently neither.

SUN 31 MAY

Went for my induction. Arrived the same time as some old guy and let him go before me. He looked like the *Dick Dastardly* character from one of dad's cartoons, thin moustache, a villain. He was part of our "double-induction". Not keen on stuff like that ever since I had to share opposite ends of a bath with a boy on school journey.

Counter girl handed each of us a *Sparkles Welcome Pack*. Backpack, water bottle, proper big towel and tiny towel. Dick Dastardly's stuff was all-blue and mine was all-pink. Grumpy git didn't offer to swap even though I let him go before me.

Some guy with *V.I.P. TRAINER* written on the back of his tight polo shirt did our induction. He put us on treadmills, pushed start, and walked off. What a millennial! I'm millennial but have the mature mind of a *Gen X*. Could see him perve at girls. Came back 20 minutes later, smiled at Dick Dastardly clinging on, then asked if I wanted to "do weights?" He apparently studied sport science at the best place in the world. I say he apparently never learned language and apparently never trained. He also mistook me for a beginner by only showing me machines. At one point he explained how to breathe. Soon as he said I was induced, I left. Wanted advice from an actual expert so I continued reading *A Portrait of Dorian Yates*. Dorian didn't study sport science. I can tell from his superior physique.

SUNDAY SUM-UP

Death is certain for the born.
For the dead, rebirth is certain.

- THE BHAGAVAD GITA

Weight: *10.3 dictionaries* (have I peaked?)

BRO

MON 1 JUN

First workout at *Sparkles*. Even though it was a Monday afternoon it was busy. Doesn't anyone work? And why are there so many girls training? Might have seen me join.

Was great to try stuff I'd seen in books like the pulleys. People call them "cables" which is illiterate but I must fit in. Tried out the calf raise. Kept waiting to be called "ballet boy" but no one did.

It will take me a while to get settled and get a plan, so won't rush. I can imagine girls saying "Oh Freddy, you're so worth the wait."

TUE 2 JUN

Gym was quiet today. Couldn't find the pullover machine I saw in Dorian's book so I asked the counter girl (scrolling phone) if they had one. Without looking up she said "We don't recommend wearing pullovers in the gym." Thought she had a fun way with words until I realized she was retarded. Then realized I was retarded for saying thanks.

WED 3 JUN

Bought a "pre-workout" at the gym. Supposed to boost energy but it boosted panic. My ears started tingling and I thought it was serious. Had to sit by the counter for ages with 999 on speed-dial. Then it must have kicked-in because I found myself trying random exercises.

There's a leg machine called the "Hack Squat" which looks like it won't hurt my back. Felt clueless without a routine so I came home and watched Dorian's documentary.

Blood & Guts was in black and white and I wanted it go color like *The Wizard of Oz*. Saw the pullover. It was disappointingly brilliant. As was Dorian's assistant who screamed "Show them Diesel!" That's a strange nick name but preferable to *Petrol* or *Hybrid*. Even when he wasn't being screamed at, Dorian pushed and pulled harder than anyone I've seen. Sister's body language book says only a genuine smile crinkles the eyes. I say only a genuine effort does stuff to the mouth area. His shows actual anguish before each rep. I had the same expression when a barbell nearly crushed my rocket.

THU 4 JUN

Had a school playground incident. I'd just found my groove on cable triceps when some blond boy bounced up and said "How many left?" I tried to process his poor grammar when another goon appeared and said "How many's he got?" He spoke like I wasn't there and dropped a belt with a chain on my foot. Said I'd be a few minutes but they both went "How - - - many - - - sets?" First I'm having to decode poor English then poor manners then do maths. Said it was my last one even though it wasn't. Then felt conscious because I was doing each arm separately and the blond boy edged closer each rep then more when I swapped arms. Soon as they heard the stack clink they swooped in. Thought I'd joined a gym. I've actually joined a jungle.

FRI 5 JUN

Text from Hugo. He's back for his work placement soon. Why would anyone voluntarily leave uni? Expect he's like dad and can't use a washing machine. His pharmacology skills might pick a good detergent though.

Had a rest from the gym. I like Fridays and don't want it spoiled by goons. Decided to laugh at them instead and searched for gym idiot videos. Found a channel called *Trap Bar*. The guy's a lawyer, lifter, and has big traps. The combo gives him a cutting sense of humor and he hates *CrossFit*. From what I can see, CrossFit is a PE class for grown-ups. The name "CrossFit" must come from the exercise style as their jolting pull-ups seem especially cross.

SAT 6 JUN

The weekend gym vibe felt different with office bods buzzing around desperate to de-chub. They looked clueless but none of the V.I.P. TRAINERs offered to help. Instead they stared at girls or their own reflection. Mainly their own reflection. I could be a V.I.P TRAINER. Or I could just be a V.I.P. Actually not if I had to keep staring at my reflection.

One guy was sat on a machine back-to-back with mine, ordering supplements from the Saint Vince man. They were called *Hulk Nation*. Bit of a silly name if you ask me. I mean why would you aspire to live in a nation that was hulked? That's like living in Bodypower. No competitive advantage in that world. Company looked dodgy, and after *HustleTech* I won't trust any brand starting with an "H". Brands with "F" and "G" can't be trusted either. F,G,H. The devil's letters.

Apart from the F in Freddy. And Fox.

SUN 7 JUN

I've now decided on a new training approach. I'll combine a basic routine with Dorian's high-intensity. I'll do 4 gym days and keep the others free for my mind. Reps will be 10 max so my un-breast-fed counting isn't confused. And I'll be dividing the body into *torso* and *limbs* as I'm on an anatomical mission.

MONDAY & THURSDAY - *TORSO*

Chest	Dumbbell bench press	2 x 10
	Pec-deck	2 x 10
Back	Front pulldown	2 x 10
	One-arm dumbbell row	2 x 6
	Dumbbell shrugs	2 x 6
Delts	Dumbbell side raise	2 x 10

TUESDAY & FRIDAY - *LIMBS*

Legs	Hack squat	2 x 10
	Leg extension	2 x 10
	Leg curl	2 x 10
Calves	Standing calf raise	2 x 10
Biceps	Standing dumbbell curl	2 x 6
Triceps	Cable one-arm pushdown	2 x 6

Hopefully people pick-up on the professional routine. Trained every day this week yet girls are still unaware of my presence. Maybe they're dedicated to their rears. V.I.P. TRAINERs view themselves front-on but girls always twist sideways to see their buttocks. Might start clapping when one checks themselves out. In one of sister's books she'd underlined a bit about the need for a supportive man.

SUNDAY SUM-UP

Care about people's approval,
And you will be their prisoner.

- THE TAO TE CHING

MON 8 JUN

First day of new routine. Took ages to find a bench but getting on back stuff was easy. Humans obsess with things they see, and what they don't see, they don't care about. Dorian must have had many mirrors growing up. I'd like to do a barbell row but my back feels dodgy. Did the one-arm version which still needs a bench.

Leaned on the dumbbell rack which annoyed the V.I.P. TRAINERs who were checking their reflection. They definitely think they're more V.I.P. than trainer.

Came home exact same time as sister and she lectured me about "playing at the gym" while we have family money worries. Then she gave me a list of jobs from her library. All depressing for a man of my IQ but there was a position in a health food store. Suppose it could be useful. I emailed them and mentioned my experience. I've eaten healthy food quite a few times.

TUE 9 JUN

First time using a hack squat. Went to use it unloaded but could still hardly move it. Doubt anyone saw but if they did they'd think my slowness was control. Had to use 2.5 kilo plates for each set. Went for water and when I came back a girl was picking up the 2.5s I'd stacked nearby. She looked up and asked if I was using them. Denied they were mine and she took them. Ended up using 5 kilo plates then felt my back twinge. Women never appreciate what I do for them. Was a relief to train arms after that but my spine still hurt on curls.

Got a reply about the job. It's not a health food store. It sells equipment, clothing and supplements. It's called *Underground Muscle* because it's part of the tube station. Got an interview on Monday. Said thanks to sister, who smiled. Females are skilfully aggressive.

WED 10 JUN

Don't have a suit so looked in dad's wardrobe. He's got whippet genes. Tried one of his old rags and it was so tight my arms felt big. I'll use it. By filling the sleeves I'll fill the employer with confidence. Dad won't even notice as his day-to-day outfit is boxer shorts. Will borrow shoes also as I've only got new pairs of *Adidas Ultraboost*. I'm saving them for a hot date. Been saving them for a while actually.

THU 11 JUN

Torso Thursday was mainly trap day as I hammered my missing muscle. Have to do shrugs by the dumbbell rack as hoisting weights around the gym floor hurts my spine.

The V.I.P. TRAINERs are getting angrier each time I block their reflection. I'm using heavier dumbbells now and my grip goes at the end of a set. Left side always goes sooner which might be from wrestling the bald-headed champ. Must persist as traps ranked 9th in the *Vogue* survey.

Looked up "best traps" and found Johnnie O' Jackson. His traps are chunks. He trains with Branch Warren, who's also massive and trains like a beast. Mr Warren got flung from a resentful, overloaded horse in *Generation Iron*. Horse riding is best left to Mr Putin.

FRI 12 JUN

Playground incident *again*. Was using cables when the lanky blond boy rolled-up. He got WAY too close and in the middle of my quality atoms said "Finished?" As I was about to answer, one of his goons said "Max, declines?" Then they all walked off and the tall one winked. The very tall are often very arrogant. Next time "Max" I shall decline to tolerate your intrusion. He's a messenger of the devil sent to stop my arms from growing. Go fork yourself.

SAT 13 JUN

Watched more *Dodge Twins*. Wonder if they've ever confused their wives? At the very least you could share a gym membership and go on alternate days. I have a problem with their stuff about girlfriend problems. Specifically, my problem is I don't have one.

SUN 14 JUN

Swung by *Sparkles* to use the steam room and glow for my interview. It was full of office bods but I detected nastiness nearby. It was Max. Vicious vibes travel through vapor. Was getting hot but refused to leave before him. Took ages because the idiot must store water in his big legs. In the end he quit before me as I've learned to endure heat from sister's greenhouse conditions.

Did some research on those who have touched Mr Sandow's leaf. All are under 6-feet tall apart from Arnold and none are Pisces. Ronnie Coleman has touched Mr Sandow's leaf 8 times in a row. Watched a video where he bench pressed 200-pound dumbbells.

And he did it with a sense of British ironic humor. He called these 14 dictionaries per side "Light weight".

SUNDAY SUM-UP

Everybody want to be a bodybuilder.
Don't nobody want to lift this heavy ass weight.

- RONNIE COLEMAN

Weight: *10.5 dictionaries!* Creatine has done something. Bit late for Bodypower.

MON 15 JUN

Went for my interview at *Underground Muscle*. Des, the manager, asked what I did in my spare time. I'd prepared for such clichés and said I read about the latest discoveries in health. Hadn't prepared for "Do you train?" I thought it was obvious. But obviously dad's suit must have toned down my torso. I recovered by saying I did train to "help my martial arts." Didn't say I quit judo after the first lesson when sister threw me on my head. Manager Des said I'd be a good fit with their "customer profile". The work is weekend only, ideal for a man of my full-time intellect.

TUE 16 JUN

Freddy Fox, *Advisor* at *Underground Muscle*, how can I help? I got it! Manager Des wants me to start Saturday. Won't even have to borrow dad's rags as I get a uniform. The real uniform is my physique but Manager Des couldn't admit that in today's cancel culture.

Went to the gym after finding out and I was buzzing. Could feel a change in the force as people were behaving differently towards me. Even the phone-scrolling counter girl said "Good evening." Then noticed something even more promising. Or someone. Just off the gym floor is a physio treatment room. And there's a slinky looking girl I've seen go in and out of there a few times. I'd like to go in and out of there a few times. Saw her slink out today, and as she locked up, she glanced my way. My confidence must be seeping out. Think sister calls it the "law of attraction". I just call it attraction.

Animal attraction.

WED 17 JUN

Finding days off from the gym hard which is weird because I hated sports years ago. Still remember the nasty boys and their non-standard use of a towel. I could have been an athlete had they not been born. Anyway they're gone now and probably all in jail or retail. *Underground Muscle* isn't retail. It's basically medical, which makes me a healthcare professional.

That got me to search for "doctor" and "muscle" and then found a YouTube channel called *Doctor Doolittle*. He's a former bodybuilder and powerlifter who flaunts a chest that pulsates every time he shouts, which is a lot. Angry pecs. Can't be all angry though as he's surrounded by animals which explains Doctor Doolittle.

Strangely, he often insists he's "not a doctor".

THU 18 JUN

The gym was so empty I begun to question whether I should be back at uni. Then I saw Max and my mojo returned. He was without his goon crew and doing squats on the *Smith Machine*. It's a vertically sliding bar with hooks that lets loners squat in safety. He was meek without his mates. Must admit his legs aren't meek. It's almost like his upper and lower body come from different species. Mongrel Max. Looks weirder in silly Fit-Fish shorts and he appears to have bought them two sizes down. I doubt it's by accident.

FRI 19 JUN

Tried the Smith Machine at the end of *limbs* workout. It's pretty good and I'm not even a loner. The empty bar weighs much less than the shame-inducing hack sled. Looked online after and was confused to see everyone hates it. They say it does all the work for you. Then saw that Chad Showcracker PhD says it's useless, so it must be good.

Hugo came back from uni. I was daydreaming out the window and saw him approach. Instead he went next door to The Patels. Sent him a text. Said he's "discussing chemistry" with Seema, Mr Patel's daughter. How dull. He has lots to learn about women.

SAT 20 JUN

First day at *Underground Muscle*. Met co-workers. Wang, a smiley, upbeat Chinese guy who doesn't appear to train but "Know number." And Steve, who seems moody and podgy. At 4 p.m. Manager Des shook my hand then went home. Staff discount on nutrition is 50%. Asked Wang why it's so high and he said sugar's cheap. The ground floor is supplements. Plus clothing, belts, wraps, even posing trunks. They look worse than Mr Sandow's leaf. Upstairs is the equipment showroom. Multi-gyms, squat racks, benches, barbells, dumbbells. Wang says it's usually deserted and I can use it whenever I want.

The work is easy. The only downsides are a lack of sunlight and a sunlight-yellow polo. Asked Steve why there were so few women customers and he said "Women are a pain." Wang said it was a rainbow-friendly store. How can it have rainbows underground? Anyway, when local girls hear about this pot of gold they'll show up.

SUN 21 JUN
FATHER'S DAY / THE LONGEST DAY

Manager Des doesn't do Sundays. Met Krzysztof Kowalski, a customer who likes to be called *KK*. When I joked that sounded like Kim Kardashian he said "I not fat. I mountain." He is a mountain, a babyface with a massive frame. He does strongman part-time and construction full-time. He asked if I found anything funny about the store so I mentioned the slight lack of women. KK told me it was "Known gay store." He then said there were "no gay" in Poland and that he didn't "mind the gay" but Polish men are "not the gay." Realized what rainbow-free meant. Lucky it was rainbow-free when he told me. He bought two fruity carb drinks and slid one to me.

Longest day today and spent it underground. Have new respect for rats. Bought a box of protein bars home for *Father's Day*. Dad took a bite and said "They hurt." Sister vultured-in and scooped them away.

SUNDAY SUM-UP

I don't eat for taste, I eat for function.

- JAY CUTLER

MON 22 JUN

The wage slavery wiped me out. Went to *Sparkles* hoping to revitalize but it was packed and all the chest stuff was taken. Just did flyes on the floor with the heaviest chrome dumbbells I could find. No pump, no feeling, no point. Sad atoms. Then did shoulders on a machine and found it felt better sitting the other way around. After a few nice reps a V.I.P. TRAINER came over and tapped me on the shoulder. He said "Respect the machine's design." For Fox sake. What about my design?

Came home and checked if there was a mountain called "KK". According to *Wikipedia*, *K2* is the world's most dangerous mountain to tackle. And only a loony would tackle KK.

TUE 23 JUN

Hugo texted from his work placement. He's at Mr Patel's pharmacy with daughter Seema. Very cosy. Asked him if they were on the same type of uni course and he said they were "on course for love."

Went to see my love and it was packed again. Scanned around and realized that most people were just scrolling on their phones. Felt like saying "Sorry, how many *likes* have you got left?"

WED 24 JUN

Decided to have a proper look at Instagram and see why it distracted people. I couldn't stand it. Comment areas were messy and full of kisses and hearts and much worse; affirmations.

The grammatically flawed *BRING IT*, the vague *NO LIMITS*, and my favorite least-favorite *GOOD VIBES ONLY* followed by hands in prayer emoticon. It gave me bad vibes only. YouTube has smarter comments and the lack of emoticons weeds out cavemen who speak in smiley. I'd never use a smiley. I love reading comments. I love the funny stuff, the weird stuff, even replies to replies.

Mitch Viola has the best comments. People mock what he does and love him at the same time. At home I just get mocked.

THU 25 JUN

Max was training alone again and training legs again. He looked at me in the mirror so I did a friendly nod. Did he reply nod? Nod he did not. Millennial mute. Why does he even train his legs so much? If he's not training them he's caressing them with a sex-toy rolling pin from top to bottom. And speaking of bottom, I'm suspicious of any men who enjoy training their backsides.

I enjoyed my own workout (chest, not glutes) as I needed dumbbells from the right end of the top rack. The racks are in three rows, which I see as three roads. The journey starts top row, top left, where it's lightest. I skipped that due to Mr Weider's home training. Then to progress, you drive right. Next up is the second row, starting left again, and heading right. Finally there's the lower rack road. If you make it all the way to the dusty right side, you've reached the sunset. You step out, lean on your car and bask in physique glory.

Got home and could just about do my anti-Chad. Could be the summer heat or it could be that food's getting annoying. Training's fun, like being with friends. But coming home to eat repeatedly must be like coming back to a woman you hate. Don't think I'll get married. I'm already in a stressful relationship with my shaker.

FRI 26 JUN

Overheard guys talking about girls in the gym. Nothing weird about that, but as a man of words, I noticed their girl-talk was in the future tense. What they were "going" to do or *who* they were "going" to do. I kept thinking, *so you haven't actually done it?* I'd never be like them and talk about a future that hadn't happened. No way. That's sad. When I get girls I'll be the campfire of true talk.

SAT 27 JUN

The store got some boxing equipment today. It's called *Slam Man*, a sort of half-man, half-dummy. You punch it and it can test reaction speed by flashing up lights. Manager Des says it's unbreakable, and that's a selling point, because if you hit people they often do break. People will buy it to beat it. Could stop divorces. It could have helped our family as mother scared dad a few times. Had to fill it with 120 litres of water which took ages with one bottle. Steve said he had a wrist injury so I did it. Strangely I saw him do wrist curls at lunch but probably rehab. Manager Des came out of his office to admire it. He said *Slam Man* represented the bulldog spirit of Great Britain. Checked that after he left. It's designed in Finland, distributed by the Dutch, and made in China.

SUN 28 JUN

Was searching for a video to check I'd built *Slam Man* right and found one of Bate Body hitting it. He must have been on fizzy water or had his once-daily magic meal because he was going nuts. KK came in and I showed him. After we closed-up he asked to have a go. He tapped it lightly and even weighing 120 kilos, *Slam Man* couldn't keep still, so I held it. The next time he hit it my wrists almost snapped. Got some wrist supports and we went again.

He then smacked it so hard two bolts flew out of *Slam Man's* head. KK stopped and said "Poland beating robot." Think he beat the adult out of me also because I felt like a child holding it. Asked Steve if he wanted a go but his wrist injury had returned.

SUNDAY SUM-UP

No pain, no gain.

- JACK LA LALANNE

Weight: *10.3 dictionaries* (What the Fox? Is the creatine faulty?)

MON 29 JUN

Snuck in the kitchen early and was making a quick shake when sister stormed in. Fumbled the shaker top and it exploded all over her. She called me a "motor moron" and screamed about being late for work. Said I didn't appreciate how disastrous it was. Did she appreciate me losing 30 grams of protein?

Eventually got to the gym and during one-arm rows I could smell something. Protein splattered around the neck of my t-shirt. Almost quit but realized many people smell like protein shakers all the time. Quite handy really as it kept people away from me while I trained. Even the V.I.P. TRAINERs couldn't get near their beloved mirrors.

TUE 30 JUN

Decided to check out the local physique standard by looking at Brit
YouTubers. Catford Koala, who I saw at Bodypower, is black, broad,
and very muscular. Everyone says he takes drugs. And *Dave Does PE*,
who's white, also very muscular, and says he takes nothing. My lizard
brain instantly disliked Dave. He reminds me of those nasty boys and
their non-standard use of a towel. And he has a shifty, on-off smile.

I can see why people think Catford Koala uses drugs. In photos, he
looks freaky. But in the videos I watched he wasn't so freaky. I kept
going back and forth between photos and video and realized it's his
broad frame and tiny waist that does it. But is there a drug for that?

Dave Does PE has a normal frame but still looks freaky. He's got
no fat on him despite doing endless Korean eating videos. And the
back of his arms look odd. Mitch Viola, and any guys who admit they
use stuff, all have a plumped-up tricep area. Like it's been filled with
water from *Slam Man*. Mine look like *Slam Man* after KK's pulverized
all the water out.

WED 1 JUL

I'm starting to notice gym people even away from the gym. It's not
carrying a protein shaker, as even chubbers who don't train use them
now. It's the clothes. If it's a girl they won't wear jeans. You can't
show-off genes in jeans. Gym girls wear tight spandex regardless of
time or location. Their gym-fabricated, fabric-covered buttocks
scream "Look at these peaches!" And if it's a guy it's all about the top
half, usually a t-shirt with the sleeve edges turned-up. This makes the
arms look bigger. And for both sexes there's a clothing cheat code.
Wear an obvious fitness brand. Sadly, that's like those guys who want
a *Ferrari* but can't afford one. So they buy a Ferrari keyring. Why
would anyone wear Fit-Fish though? It's trying way too hard. The best
clothing to show you're part of gym culture is a good body. And
Adidas.

THU 2 JUL

Kreed from *More Curls, More Girls* despite having no videos on arms
has arms that look curvy in a sweatshirt.

You know you've made it when you wear normal clothes but look abnormal. I can't even look abnormal with the sleeve turn-up trick. It improved my arms but exposed my womb-stolen brachialis. If I avoid people sideways they might not notice, though it would take a lot of planning for the gym.

FRI 3 JUL

Had a rubbish *limbs* workout. First my arms were under threat of extinction and today it's my legs. Went home and searched for "best legs ever". Someone called Tom Platz kept coming up. His legs didn't look like legs especially from behind. I read he once squatted with one plate a side for half an hour. I can't do one plate for half a second. Typed in "tom platz steroids" to see if he claimed powered-by-nature like Dirk O' Flynn. He did not.

Also watched a video where he asked other pro bodybuilders about drugs. They pixelated their faces apart from one guy, who according to comments, was Lee Priest. He's Australian, and as they descend from English criminals, they didn't bother with pixels. Lee and me have opposite problems. His limbs outpace his torso and by a lot. Instead of two arms it's like he's got four legs. I'm starting to worry that genes really are a thing. I hope not. Or I'm destined to become a bullying, critical, family-breaker. With small arms. And small legs. And no calves.

SAT 4 JUL
1776 - INDEPENDENCE DAY (USA)

Spent most of the day prepping for a stock take tomorrow. Kept checking phone to avoid the stress. What I saw stressed me more. Social media was a sea of Fit-Fish. Despite being British they were sucking-up and celebrating *Independence Day*. And they were asking "What do you love about our brand?" The clowns who responded were already dressed in their gear yet wanted even more attention. That's like hoping to get married by wearing a wedding ring.

And who designed their awful logo, Stevie Wonder? They're like *Tesla*. People mention them but no one stops to think clearly and go "My god, that's an ugly baby."

SUN 5 JUL

Did the stock-take which meant counting every item on every shelf. Kept making errors. Wang could tell I'd never been breast-fed because he let me go early and he sent Steve home as he needed feeding.

Went by *Sparkles*. Got changed and came out onto the gym floor thinking how decent Wang was. Started my workout and noticed Max and friend filming. Said to myself I'd be like Wang, spread joy. Max was squatting and I wanted to use the leg extension nearby. Waited until he wasn't recording and asked if it was okay to use it. He said "Can you just not interrupt?" I walked off with a fake smile even though he'd poisoned the gym's atmosphere. Couldn't train after. No wonder my legs are struggling.

2 a.m. Max is every bully from my past, every reason for my heart pounding. He has a smiling, smug face I dream of bashing with a bat but then back-off from in reality. Except next time I won't retreat. I'll step up, stand up, and make his head a home run.

SUNDAY SUM-UP

Everybody pities the weak. Jealousy, you have to earn.

- ARNOLD SCHWARZENEGGER

MON 6 JUL

Was enjoying *torso* day, dumbbell benching, when a guy next to me finished a set. He re-racked his dumbbells and changed them for a heavier pair. He sat down, looked at me, and then looked around me. I thought he was looking for a friend. A minute later he got up and asked a stranger for help. I'd been dismissed! I'd become a book judged by its cover even though the cover was capable. I watched his set in the mirror. It was a crap range of motion and he had to keep thrusting his pelvis. The helper guy sucked-up by saying "All you" every shaky rep when he should have accurately said "Mainly me". In just five minutes I'd witnessed discrimination, terrible technique, and imprecise use of the English language.

TUE 7 JUL

Training was flat today. Later on I realized it was gym PTSD from the dismissive Max and the dismissive pelvis-thruster. The British are sneery at times. Kept replaying both incidents and could only break my thoughts by finding American YouTubers. I don't care about fake upbeatness as it's better than genuine sneer. Mitch Viola always makes me smile especially when I hear the music in his videos. Some fans call it the "Natty Anthem". It's awful but awfully addictive. A few people say bad stuff about him yet he has a fun life. He trains, he meets people, and he drives nice cars at night while cruising for calories. And he's got a new girlfriend. I haven't even got an old one. He keeps saying "Right babe?" to her. Not sure she is the right babe. Or is that me being sneery now? Better stop or the universe will punish me with the opposite life. I'll end up not training, not knowing anyone, and I'll ride on buses at night saying "No babe. No babe. No babe."

WED 8 JUL

Spent all day online. Watched Menial Jerks and realized not all Brits are sneery. Then found an American who was. He's called *Gym Stop* and has a PhD like Chad. Geeks are one-dimensional but Gym Stop fancies himself and is covered in the dirtiest of dirty marks. He also has a supplement range. So many people use science to sell stuff. I'd prefer someone to write "This might work" on a tub. Stopped looking at Gym Stop and found someone who doesn't hide behind science. He uses brute strength. His name is *Wally Reels*. He laughs like Zeus and must be powered by him. Watched him warm-up on the bench with two plates a side. The bar moved like a hot spoon through Mitch Viola's *Ben & Jerry's*. If I could do two plates for one rep my ego would explode. Watching Wally is like having a dream where I'm doing something athletic. Then I wake up and can't open the new toothpaste.

THU 9 JUL

Decided to bike to the gym as it was sunny, and I arrived the same time as Max, on a motorbike.

He acted cool even though there's nothing cool about wearing shorts on a motorized vehicle. Bet he only has a motorbike to reveal his legs. Some girls who came out of the gym glanced at his motorbike but ignored my *Trek* (10 gears). He thought he was even cooler to ignore the girls looking.

During my workout I walked by him and he was studying an *iPad*. Thought it was gay porn then realized it was a bodybuilding show. It's quite hard to tell upside down especially as the men had hands on their hips like human teapots. Max's goons said "You gonna do it?" I wondered what "it" was? Their vague use of English is infuriating when I'm trying to spy. Then some Euro house music started playing and they danced across the gym floor swinging their arms above their heads. Sister's dancer friend once told me that men must never dance with their arms overhead. She was right.

FRI 10 JUL

Was doing the standing calf raise and heard Max and goons again. With my back turned they didn't suspect surveillance. Max was looking at a "physique" show yesterday. He must think he's good enough to reveal himself. Found out there are three categories of bodybuilding competition. First there's *bodybuilding*, Arnold and Dorian, big guys. Then there's *classic*. That's all about having good lines. The guys can also be big, but to prevent them being too big, there are height and weight cut-offs. And speaking of cut-offs, there's *physique*. These guys have their legs cut-off by wearing surf shorts, supposedly to make them regular guys on a beach. But they're still ultra-muscular and I've never seen anyone like that in public. Most near-naked people (apart from at Bodypower) look like blobs.

SAT 11 JUL

Exhausting day at *Underground Muscle*. Feet broken. Working with the public is highly overrated. If I was a poet my feet wouldn't hurt. Felt jealous of Hugo as he's still in education. Then later I realized we're in the same business. I help people to not get sick and he helps if they do. Not sure what's better.

Asked Wang more about himself today and he said "Mud blood", Harry Potter for mixed race. In his case, Chinese mother, Irish dad.

His dad's surname is *Kerr* which means his full name is *Wang Kerr*. Repeated it out loud but he still looked confused. Thought only Americans didn't know the word. Thought I'd upset him so switched to culture and asked if he'd read the Chinese *Tao Te Ching*. Wang said "Only buy British."

SUN 12 JUL

Noticed customers who buy vitamins look unhealthy and customers who buy supplements look skinny. Not sure if people look rubbish then buy stuff to fix it, or if they buy stuff then look rubbish? If I stop it all will I look healthy and muscular? Actually, dad disproves it.

Tomorrow's pay day so before we closed I spent the last bit of my uni loan on creatine and a herb called *Tribulus Terrestris*. Wang said "Make body girl want." Steve said "Girls never want you." After a week of insults, I didn't ask whether he meant men in general or me.

SUNDAY SUM-UP

When people see some things as beautiful,
Other things become ugly.

- THE TAO TE CHING

Weight: *10.4 dictionaries*

MON 13 JUL

Got my first pay check. Went out and bought a spanking new pair of all-black *Adidas Ultraboosts*. Then went to the gym and asked counter girl if she could keep them in the office. She actually asked if I was going to wear them! Girls. She asked what was wrong with the lockers. Had to explain they were valuable and only to be used on special occasions. She realized I was right eventually.

Kept thinking what would happen if the staff stole them. In the end no one did and I got them back to the Fox-hole. They're safe from dad because despite being skinny he has fat feet. And sister could never admit being my size and thus could never take them. Girls lie about their feet. Some keep their size more secret than their phone number. I've known many girls who wouldn't tell me either.

TUE 14 JUL

Was resting on the hack squat when a girl came up and asked to take some 20 kilo plates nearby. Was happy she thought they were mine. Then she picked up both at once, and against a bench, did barbell hip thrusts with 3 plates a side. 140 kilos! 300 pounds! 21.4 dictionaries! Was transfixed by her thrusting yet repulsed by her power. Sister's book calls it *cognitive dissonance*. I call it confusion.

None of the girls here are confused though. They're on a mission to beautify their behinds. Some girls aim to get rid of junk in the trunk. The soggy glutes. Then there are girls who master every buttock-buster known to woman. They're glutesmiths. They lunge, leg press, and they do all kinds of squat. Quarter, half, sissy, and full. Never seen them do the hack squat. It's too manly and that's why I was drawn to it. They might use the adductor if no one's perving. Hardly see them on leg curls and never on extensions. Quit the quads and hold the hams to maximize your maximus. Speaking of Max, he's the only male I've ever seen using the adductor.

WED 15 JUL

Keep seeing the old boy who did the double-induction with me, Dick Dastardly. He struts around puffed-up like he's carrying carpet rolls under each arm. Either he works in a carpet store or he has an inferiority complex. Plus, soon as he arrives at the gym and before he gets changed, he goes over to the leg press and puts a towel on it. Brits put towels on hotel sun loungers to annoy the Germans but this is a gym. And he puts a towel on his *next* exercise. I watched him put a towel on the leg press to look like he was using it, then he went off and did four sets of extensions. I'd never have the arrogance to do that. Plus I don't think *Nemo* has the right image.

THU 16 JUL
NEW MOON

Can hardly write. I was about to try barbell shrugs in a rack when Max and goons beat me to the space. So I did something else while they did deadlifts and filmed themselves. Max got to 3 plates for an over-dramatic set of screamers. After the last rep he unbuckled his fashion belt and flung it down.

The belt has his name on it, more self-promotion. When they finished and I approached he said to his goons "He'll need them off", referring to the plates. Wasn't sure if they were still filming and still arrogant so I said to leave them on. Then instead of unloading it, I deadlifted Max's max. It went up okay because I felt them watching, but when I placed it onto the rack with control, something pinged. Felt like my spine was shot by an arrow. Then it hurt to even wiggle the collars off. I had to fake a phone call, get my bag, and go home. Sister saw me hobbling in and asked what I'd done. When I told her she said it was due to the new moon and sun combining. More like the ego and gravity combining. What a Fox-up.

FRI 17 JUL

In total agony. It's almost summer and I'm almost in crutches. Couldn't go to the gym and someone's broken our shower which means the universe must want me to rest.

Watched YouTube the whole day. Saw a guy called *Fictus Pondus* which sounds Latin but he's seems Latino. He's heavily built and lifts heavily. I don't know if it was the angle I was watching, tucked up in bed, but his weights seemed to defy gravity. Then got depressed thinking I'd never defy gravity again.

Then I watched a video of Ronnie Coleman and he was in a wheelchair. I felt much better.

2 a.m. Trashed the Tribulus. Hasn't made any girls notice me.

SAT 18 JUL

Almost didn't make it into work. Manager Des wasn't around so I phoned *Sparkles* to freeze my membership. Counter girl said I'd need a doctor's note. Why does everyone ask for a doctor's note? Pretended I didn't have a doctor. Then she asked if I'd considered the gym physio and gave me her number. She could be the slinky one who looked. But would she like me less as a cripple?

6 p.m. Called the physio. Her name's Alexa but she prefers "Lexy". When I first heard sister's name I felt the repulsion of accidentally seeing gay porn. Had planned 1 session but signed-up for 10 after she said "Your body is priceless." I knew she'd been watching.

2 a.m. Tried to retrieve Tribulus from trash but already gone.

SUN 19 JUL

Stopped by the gym after work to test how crippled I was. Only managed chrome dumbbells.

Came back and watched *Fictus Pondus* to inspire my return to heavy training. Then YouTube showed videos that said his weights weren't real. In one clip, a big blond called *No Bulky Teen* got in Fictus's face. It was like one of those undercover consumer shows. *No Bulky Teen* must have bulky balls to confront such a muscular man but some people don't like what he does. I reckon he's justified. The public think bodybuilders are weak. Even dad thinks he's stronger. And if he heard about *Fictus Pondus* he'd be smug forever.

How do fake weights get into gyms? There's only one explanation. Counter girls. They scroll, they question nothing, and they have very low IQs. Why haven't I approached one?

SUNDAY SUM-UP

Light weight, yeah buddy.

- RONNIE COLEMAN

MON 20 JUL

Decided to workout but a Monday gym is no place for the crippled.
People brushed by unaware that even a slight nudge sent shockwaves
through my spine. I probably looked up for a fight as I couldn't get out
of people's way like normal.

Training torso was a joke. Couldn't do dumbbell bench because
hoisting the dumbbells hurt. And everything twinged doing back.
Couldn't do side raises for shoulders but my penthouse genetics
allowed for temporary deltoid deletion.

Feeling all the pain made me resentful about Max. Why was he
filming that day? Bet he's like most of the mirror-loving gym clowns.
In love with themselves.

TUE 21 JUL

He is in love with himself. I had to look Max up. Was easy to find as
he'd tagged himself everywhere. 20,000 followers! Jesus did
considerably more and only had 12.

The nerve of this guy. Says he's a "Hypertrophy & Aesthetics"
specialist. More hype than trophy. And what's aesthetic about legs like
elephants? Bet he thinks *MAX POWER* is a clever brand name. He
also tagged Fit-Fish everywhere. Think tags were designed to help
others find topics but now they just help narcissists get found.

What even qualifies someone to be an online coach other than being
shirtless, shameless, and ruthless? He truly is a walking cliché. At least
he's walking.

WED 22 JUL

First physio session with Lexy. Moron Max came out of her treatment
room as I went in! She noticed us staring and asked me if we knew
each other. Couldn't say I hated the clown so I deflected by
mentioning the dodgy deadlift. She said I should have been more
careful as "Max Power is *very* strong in the legs." That's his actual
name. Ridiculous. Why did she even have to say it? Why stab my self-
esteem? Talk about adding insult to spinal injury. And if he's so great,
why was he in here? She did lots of tests, prodded around, then asked
if I'd consider yoga. Yoga!

She'd just come back from "rolling the mat" in some local-yokel "uber chilled class". I hid my disgust. She looks very flexible. *Flexy-Lexy*. She gave me rehab exercises to do but they'll be trashed. She's going to massage my spine next session. Will I have to take my shirt off? Maybe she likes me. She clearly has good taste in men. Some men.

THU 23 JUL

Managed to get out of bed without cursing. Was thinking about Fictus Pondus. His weights might be fake but his body's real. What matters more, muscles or integrity? I never hear girls saying they want to grab a guy's integrity.

Got to the gym for torso but couldn't do much. Gave me a chance to observe everyone. I noticed that during a set no one smiled. Runners never smile either. I know exercise takes effort but some movements are enjoyable. Plus I reckon smiling is good for the body chemistry. Arnold constantly smiled in *Pumping Iron*. I'll start smiling and see what it does. Only at the gym though.

2 a.m. What if Flexy does want me to take my shirt off? Might need to make her dislike me until I'm ready. Better not smile at her.

FRI 24 JUL

Remembered to smile during my workout. Just so happened to do it when I was testing out the adductor. Smiled at a girl as she glanced in the rocket's direction. Saw her leave the gym without a smile.

Then decided to shower at the gym while the home one's fixed. Terrible timing. Thought some guy confused the shower for the toilet when I saw liquid trickle under his cubicle to mine. Looked down and saw a shaker on its side. He was drinking his shake in the shower. While it's good to go anti-Chad, this guy's respect for the anabolic window made me want to chuck him out of one.

SAT 25 JUL

Manager Des had body fat testing scales delivered today. They're made in Japan, the place where no one's fat. We're charging £1 for customers to measure their shame. I had a go and was 22%.

Everyone online is 5%. Wang made me feel better as he was 24%. Steve said they were a "gimmick for girls" and wouldn't go on them. He's like mother. Manager Des said he didn't get to where he was in life by measuring body fat. He left while eating a donut.

Looked up lean bodybuilders. Andreas Munzer kept showing up. Most bodybuilders are known for good body parts but he was known for being shredded. His skin looked like a paper cut could wipe him out. And wiped out he was, at 31. He'd been using *diuretics*, drugs which flush away water so muscles look *Marvel*. But they also flush away stuff that keeps the heart ticking. Google's cheery algorithm then showed me stories of bodybuilders dying. Most headlines said "STEROIDS" but none of the deaths seemed to be directly from that. Journalists must have learned to write on the fiendish forum.

SUN 26 JUL

Body fat now 24%. On target to be 100% in 38 days. Steve peered over my shoulder and laughed. Laugh at my figures, dough boy, and I'll just laugh at your figure.

Continued looking up top shred bodybuilders which became top dead bodybuilders. Then I read about a guy who died at 22. That's next year and the Sunday doom almost smothered me. Almost.

His name was Aziz Shavershian. He was a skinny gamer kid who joined the fiendish forum asking for advice under the name *Zyzz*. He then sold his beloved *World of Warcraft* account to pay for a gym membership. Within 3 years he transformed his body from not noticeable to not ignorable. And, not being gay, but apart from a few dirty marks, he had a beautiful physique. This was 2007, before social media took off, yet he filmed everything. He did festivals, he danced like a donut, and he partied with friends and girls. At first I thought it was cringe but then realized that was other people's sneeriness speaking for me so I dropped it. And I could see why he changed other people's minds. His antics said *it's okay to pursue this lifestyle*. The only downside is he sparked copycats like Fit-Fish. His message was to be yourself but ironically they're all about fitting-in.

In the Spring of 2011 he was shifting away from the wild stuff and going towards being a straight-up motivator. Sadly, that summer he died without warning.

An autopsy showed, unknown to him, that he was born with a heart defect. And also unknown to him was that in dying, he would inspire an entire generation.

SUNDAY SUM-UP

Don't be afraid of being different.
Be afraid of being the same as everyone else.

- ZYZZ

Weight: *10.6 dictionaries* (thanks Zyzz!)

MON 27 JUL

Shame central. Was doing one-arm rows and to save my spine I rested the dumbbell on a bench between sets. On the way back from getting water someone banged the bench. The dumbbell dropped off and rolled along the floor fast. I tried to catch it but it went into the back of Dick Dastardly's achille's tendon as I reached him. He spun around and screamed "BASTARD" at my face. *The whole gym looked.* I said sorry so many times. He said he already had an injury and this would be painful. Not as painful as it was for me.

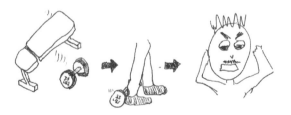

2 a.m. Being born 6 weeks before parents got married, I'm literally a bastard, but no need for Dick Dastardly to be so figurative.

TUE 28 JUL

My workout got distracted by thinking about Flexy-Lexy tomorrow. She's quite tall, maybe taller while my back's busted. Found videos about dating the taller woman but they all copy and pasted wishy-washy tips like being "okay with yourself". I have much better ideas.

Men should take women on *horizontal* dates. Drives, bus rides, boats, restaurants. And always at night. It's hard to judge height in the dark. A drive at night would be especially good. If you meet in the gym to do cardio, pick the sit-down bike. The cross-trainer can even make you taller at certain points in the stride. Once off equipment, keep moving like a boxer to avoid comparison. If you do this long enough, they'll see past any exterior limitations, fall in love, and you end up horizontal in the best way possible. Oh, and getting too muscular makes anyone appear shorter. Not got that problem yet.

WED 29 JUL

Session number two with Flexy-Lexy and she *didn't* ask me to take my t-shirt off. I laid face down on a chair thing while she spent 45 minutes doing micro movements around my spine. Must be tiring so her endurance must be powered by attraction. There was no music, no oils, and no talking. Actually at one point she asked if everything was okay. I nodded. And in my head I added "But you'd like it more if I was facing the other way." She's lucky I'm a gentleman out-loud.

2 a.m. Concerned about the dominance hierarchy being flipped when I lie down on the chair thing. It's only for now though.

THU 30 JUL
1947 - ARNOLD SCHWARZENEGGER BORN

Shower was still broken and I refused to feminize myself by having a bath. Was in a bad mood and hoped the gym would let me forget my domestic frustrations.

Got half way through a decent workout when I saw the allegedly injured Dick Dastardly doing standing calf raises with the whole stack. 600 lbs. Even though he was moving it just *one inch* where was the "achilles injury"? One-inch Dick.

FRI 31 JUL

Feel violated. Plumber cancelled but thought I could get away without showering for one more day. Stepped out of the house, felt the heat, and knew I'd need one if I was going to train properly. Already had gym bag but rushed back in to grab *Sparkles* backpack which came with a towel.

Had killer session then headed for shower. Grabbed backpack and went to the shower dressed. Took off gym gear, slung it over shower door. Gym gear dropped on the wet floor but backpack was hooked inside the cubicle. Kept enjoying shower. Finished shower and opened backpack. No big towel, only the tiny wash cloth. Felt like those dreams where I walked to school naked. But this was actually happening so I had to decide which side got the tiny covering-up resources. Held wash cloth over rocket, other palm over the rear, and crept out of cubicle. Almost made it to my locker when Max showed up, stopped, and KEPT STARING. Almost threw my arms up in rage but realized the inevitable wardrobe malfunction. Eventually he walked into the toilets and I got dressed.

Where the hell did my big towel go? And how dare that idiot stare? If I was an actress I'd sue.

SAT 1 AUG

Still traumatized at work. Told KK what happened and he said if I want "To be mens, train with mens!" then he mentioned *The Iron Pit*. So it does exist even if their telephone answering skills don't.

Might consider it after my recent exposure although it's an all-male gym. KK doesn't train there but used to. He uses construction work to maintain the mountain. Without his protection it could be like me going to jail and becoming the jackpot.

The exposure theme continued when I saw Manager Des getting changed before he went home. Now I know why he won't go on the scales. I felt bad being a cherub but he's a statue of jello. Can't believe how office clothes hide the sins of a sandwich. Only needs Fit-Fish for his fake public profile to be complete.

Found out that sister had stolen my towel. She assumed it wasn't being used because it was pink. How dare women complain about equality! Bet it was for a *Sick Abs Fast* workout. Imagine I stole your bra, sis, and used it for assisting my pull-ups.

SUN 2 AUG

Met another regular who everyone calls Terror Turk. He'd just come back from there (Turkey, not terror) and used to help KK on construction. Not sure if he's legal but I decided it was rude to ask. Instead he asked me if "Man Des" was around which I assumed meant Manager Des. Soon as I shook my head he ripped open his 1970s shirt, shouted "YES MAN!" and walked up to the equipment showroom. He then trained shirtless and sometimes he growled. No wonder the showroom's deserted. After he finished he said if "Anyone give you trouble, I smash their skull." Should have pointed to Steve's skull.

Did some Dorian research later. His dad was a pilot and his mother rode horses, a perfect genetic combo of science and nature. My dad used to be a tour operator and my mother's never worked. What does that create? Someone who watches others fly-off or stays at home doing nothing. I'm born to be a spectator only.

SUNDAY SUM-UP

All else being equal, the guy with the best genetics will have the best physique. But rarely are all things equal.

- DORIAN YATES

MON 3 AUG

Sister jumped in the fixed shower first and I went to the gym angry. Typical Monday and waited ages for a cable. Finally got one then noticed a lost-looking kid nearby so I offered to share. Did my set and went for water. Walking back I saw Max plus goons stroll up and drop stuff around the kid's feet, *mid-set*. Fashion belts, bottles, man-bags. The intimidation of imbeciles. The kid stopped his set and I heard Max say the same crap he said to me. "How many left?" I kept thinking, if you don't stand for something, you fall for everything. Before the kid could answer Max, I did. They turned and I said "We're doing high-volume based on Chad Showcracker's latest research." They just stared so I added "With timed 30-second rests." I held my up *G-Shock* watch and didn't blink. I learned that from sister's body language book. After what felt like ages the Fit-Fish bullies swam off! Did extra sets to block them from a sneaky return.

Think you can barge your way through people, Max? Think you can drop your belt and people's self-esteem? Not on my watch, weasel. Next time I'll say I'm doing Mitch Viola's *8-hour arms*.

TUE 4 AUG

Saw Max in the gym and wondered how he manages to call himself a coach. He doesn't even coach anyone in person.

Had to know if that was actually weird so searched famous coaches. Some Middle-Eastern looking guy called *Hard Man Boy* came up. He spoke well but looked a slob. Sorry, but the proof is in the pudding, not being one. And in Gold's Gym Venice, a guy called *Chuck Perspex* barely goes beyond Max. Chuck's clients do train in the gym but he just touches them randomly. I've heard Hollywood people like being touched randomly. Both these guys train pro bodybuilders but I don't see how you call yourself pro if you can't train yourself? It's like saying you're a world champion at tying shoe-laces when your mother does it for you.

People on the fiendish forum say it's normal to have a coach. Well, I'd rather not be normal. I'd rather be Dorian because he didn't have a coach. Bet I can spot people with coaches now. They'll be the ones with their laces untied.

WED 5 AUG

Third session with Flexy. Was expecting another massage but she asked me to show her the rehab stuff she gave me, the stuff I trashed. Because of my high-capacity cortex I remembered enough to convince her. One was a standing hip-thrust and that was difficult because of the thoughts. She actually said I was making progress! Physios exist because people want company, but in this case she wants my company. As I left she said "Keep it up, you're amazing." Knew it wouldn't take long for the Fox charm to woo her.

Double-checked to see if Dorian had a coach. He didn't. But he was influenced by the ideas of Mike Mentzer, a bodybuilder who put high-intensity on the map. Mike should have touched Mr Sandow's leaf in 1980 but Arnold touched it first. Mr Mentzer got his influence from Arthur Jones, an uber-masculine scientist of intensity. Mr Jones invented the *Nautilus* machines. The threads of intelligence that run from Jones to Mentzer to Dorian explain a lot. The threads that run loose from dad's boxers explain even more.

THU 6 AUG

The gym was dead so I used the focus for super-strict laterals. Got such a pump I had to pull up my sleeves. My shoulders looked suspiciously good. Only say suspicious because people say good shoulders come from steroids. Something about that area having greedy receptors to suck up the drugs. Same for traps. Sounds like broscience to me. Five months into training and my traps look worse than my mother's. But my shoulders even shock me. They shocked another guy also. Didn't seem nasty but stared a nanosecond too long. That's in sister's body language book. I suppose gyms are the modern art gallery and I'm now a popular exhibit.

Found a *More Curls, More Girls* video on shoulders. His are still bowling balls. Mine are more golf. Or tennis when pumped.

FRI 7 AUG

Sister came home and was slamming everything. It's pre-birthday panic. Every Fox has it apart from mother who claims to get younger every year. Dad always says "Another one down the drain."

I don't think he'd blow-up on *Instagram*. Asked sister what was wrong and she went more mental. Said if I didn't start every question with "Alexa" she'd start calling me Frederick again. Such a low blow. It's taken me years to rid myself of a three-syllable name. If I'd been Jack or Zack or a Troy, I might not have even needed a good body.

SAT 8 AUG

Met a friendly customer today, Otis. In his words he's a "Black, black-taxi driver." Said once he qualified as a cabbie he started getting out of shape. He looked like he's been out of shape since the car was invented. Then he said he wanted to "muscle up". I suggested cutting down on body fat first but he said that could wait until summer. I thought August was summer. He started looking at Manager Des's *Triple Threat* special. It's a protein, pre-workout, and pre-bed combo for less cash. I said a pre-workout might be dodgy when driving and hinted that a protein powder could double-up as a pre-bed shake. He was too Newbie-inspired to listen so I shut up. He measured his body fat at 28%. That was bad and then he asked "Is that good?" I said it was good.

Bought a selection of herbal teas for sister's birthday tomorrow. They're almost out-of-date but girls don't mind about things like that. I contemplated getting her protein but she's solid already.

SUN 9 AUG

Sister's birthday. Did the usual family thing, made a card. Had left it last-minute as still resented the threat to call me Frederick. Was rushing for work so I folded a piece of paper and scribbled a joke.

Front: *What do you say when your sister's upset?*

Inside: *Are you having a crisis?*

She opened it and cried. Handed her the herbal teas and she cried more. Said she was allergic. Took them off her. Overheard her on the phone to a friend saying she's "waiting for Mr Right". Almost got out the door when I heard "Get me protein."

Tried to make friendly conversation with Steve. Asked what protein he recommended for girls and he said "You don't know any." Technically incorrect. And in time, many millions will know me.

SUNDAY SUM-UP

Do you have the patience to wait 'til your mud settles,
And the water is clear?

- THE TAO TE CHING

Weight: *10.5 dictionaries* (will stop pre-workouts)

MON 10 AUG

Felt zonked after spending hours online last night. It's disrupting my proper life balance as I now spend more time looking at others than at myself.

It seems lots of people are looking at Max. In less than a month he's gone from 20,000 to 25,000 loser-followers. And he's started describing himself using *we* when it's only him. He even refers to himself in the third person. "Max loves his growing legion of fans!" Of course they're growing when you use multiple versions of yourself. Why would someone do that? Watched lots of Dorian interviews and not once did I hear him mention "team". Probably because there wasn't one. Probably because he knows it's manly to be a lone wolf. Only sheep would say "We're happy with the result." "We smashed it." "We nailed it."

If I hear another snowflake bigging themselves up I'M going to smash their man-bag and then I'LL nail it to the Smith Machine.

TUE 11 AUG

Was on *limbs* day and I wanted to use the calf machine but there was a guy leaning on it for ages. And because he had massive calves I waited ages. Eventually asked him and he wasn't using it. He was praying. His name is Colin and he's a priest. He apologized many times. Never heard a priest apologize before. Told him I thought because of his big calves he was using the machine and having a rest. He looked down, looked confused, then said he's never trained them.

Then I was confused. Don't think a man of God would lie, especially not a man in sandals. *Colin Calves.*

Got back thinking about Max's "fans". They annoyed me so I went looking for other platforms. There are endless physiques on *TikTok*. It's like Instagram and YouTube had a baby and the baby came out retarded. It's full of crazy *before* and *after* transformations. I reckon if anyone records insane progress they knew it would happen. And I reckon in a generation without confidence, that certainty only comes from one thing. It's not *HustleTech.*

2 a.m. Forgot it's dad's birthday tomorrow. Woke up to see if anyone famous is born the same day to put as trivia in his card. There isn't. Joe Rogan's birthday today though, same year as dad. Thinks he's tough with all his ninjitsu and hunting and eating elk. Says hunting's natural and fair. Hardly a fair fight to take out Bambi with a *Glock*. Rogan must be like dad so I could take him out. That wouldn't be a fair fight though as I'm a much younger, nimbler, and manlier man.

WED 12 AUG

Flexy-Lexy was smiley today and biologically girls can't smile unless they mean it. I didn't see her smiling as I was face-down but I could tell from her voice. She said my legs were firmer. Were they soft before? Think legs were top-10 in the *Vogue* survey but I dismissed them. I know why women like legs. Women hate their own chunky legs, so if they stand near a man who's even chunkier, they feel better. Men with big legs must be like an instant diet. Tom Platz must be like lipo.

Went by *Underground Muscle* to get dad an inspiring present. Bought him a big tub of *Weider Mega Mass 2000* weight gainer. Embarrassing getting it home on the tube as it wouldn't fit in a bag. Draped my arms over it like an ape but people still stared. Got in and gave it to him. He said "Don't like milkshakes. Your mother likes milkshakes. Thanks, son." Put it in the kitchen cupboard. Decided I won't have children.

Saw videos of Joe Rogan training. He's not like dad. He's got a beast body and knows martial moves that could cancel out my day of judo. Probably have a chance if I borrowed his *Glock*.

THU 13 AUG

The protection of *Sparkles* is shattered. Mother's new male, Sin, came into the gym. I hid in the aerobics studio and checked the photo mother texted. Definitely him. Definitely a dweeb. Was angry he was in my gym, angry mother said he had a great body but I didn't, and angry I'd abandoned my workout. It's like quitting the bald-headed champ after introducing him to the outdoors arena. Had to watch Dirk O' Flynn after as he had tons of workout footage and needed a substitute. Sometimes he trains in the middle of the night. Must be when duck eggs hatch.

2 a.m. Mental. Thought about Dirk's 4 a.m. workouts then got annoyed about Sin ruining mine. Got dressed and got a bus to *Sparkles*. Place was empty apart from a cleaner with big arms. Got an amazing pump from being full of carbs. More amazing was seeing Otis waddle in. He'd just finished dropping-off his last passenger. I was shocked to see how big he's got and more shocked when he asked why he hadn't seen me here before at this time. When we finished he gave me a lift home in his taxi. Felt the cab lean even when it wasn't cornering.

FRI 14 AUG

Dragged myself to the gym despite being there 12 hours before. The only people in were some guys taking out one of the leg presses. Plus Dick Dastardly who swarmed around repeating "Utter disgrace". Don't know why as there's still another one to put his towel on. I smiled at the guys for solidarity and they said they'd be back tomorrow with something new.

Was getting changed after and saw someone emerge from the showers. Looked away but my mind imprinted the image. Not being gay, but couldn't ignore the absence of rocket boosters. And the guy was young. According to *More Curls, More Girls* if you use a chemical cheat code, Mother Nature's boosters go into hiding. But according to Mitch Viola, if the rocket hangs lower than the boosters, it's a good thing. Has something to do with proportions. Either way, no one's judging mine yet.

SAT 15 AUG

Spending too much of my wages at the place I earn them. Like buying a pre-workout at lunch due to boredom.

Went to the gym after to see their new leg machine. It's a *Pendulum Squat*, a shoulder pad attached to a long lever on a pivot, like lifting one end of a bridge. Tried it unloaded but it was still embarrassingly heavy. Bought second pre-workout of the day from gym counter and tried again. Added one plate. Isaac Newton has lots to answer for because I got stuck in the bottom position. The Very Important Personal Trainers didn't think me being crushed was very important and walked by. Had to bend my knees 'til they touched my chest so the safety pin could take the weight. Slithered out and sprawled flat. Dick Dastardly walked over me and flicked a blue *Sparkles* towel that should have been mine. My head was pulsating from pre-workout. I'd gone supplemental.

SUN 16 AUG

Work was quiet so I tried *TikTok* again. It's full of boys who look like Bieber and girls who look like they could bash Bieber up. Plus people trying to be *Wally Reels* with some unbalanced lift that's hard to measure and thus hard to compare. That's why kettlebells are popular. People should balance their fragile egos instead. People will do anything to be famous. Anything but work hard.

Met Colin Calves again at the gym. Said he was there to "worship at the other temple." Thought he meant Dorian's gym for a sec. Colin says God wants us to be strong. Never knew he took such an interest. I liked hearing his sermon but I'm starting to think Sparkles is the wrong place for improving my God-given gifts. Instead of training with Lee Priest, I'm training with an actual priest.

SUNDAY SUM-UP

In order to lead the orchestra, first turn your back to the crowd.

- MIKE MENTZER

MON 17 AUG

Thought all weekend about whether to stay at the gym and I decided it's impossible to sparkle at *Sparkles*. Will train today and ask about leaving tomorrow. Always best to ask for what you want on a Tuesday. Mondays make monsters.

Speaking of monsters, found a YouTuber called *Cyclops*. In Greek mythology, Cyclops had one eye, but this geezer sees everything. And he hates Fit-Fish. Even I didn't realize some stuff about them until I watched his videos. As Cyclops is a cool chap it makes my views of Fit-Fish even more rational. And it's confirmed I must escape this shark tank.

TUE 18 AUG

Didn't realize I'd signed up for *Guantanamo Bay*. Spoke to the manager about leaving and he said although the fees are monthly, it's a 12-month contract. So the earliest time to go is after the 13th month. That doesn't even make sense. Contracts exist to punish those with flexible minds.

Came home and read a 1985 study in sister's book which said being caged with rivals causes severe drops in testosterone. 1985 is also when Arnold wrote his encyclopedia. Unlike Arnold who's "coming in the gym" and "coming at home", I'm caged in the gym and stressed at home. Bet I have the testosterone of a two-year-old.

WED 19 AUG

Flexy-Lexy likes mongrel Max! He was leaving her treatment room before my session and I heard her say "Keep it up, you're amazing." That's what she said to me! After I went in she kept talking about him *as* she prodded me. Max this, Max that. Every prod combined with a compliment was a virtual violation. I thought men were supposed to be the insensitive ones.

Got in and watched *Pumping Iron* to cheer up. Then read *Sparkles Terms & Conditions*. Section 11, *Your right to cancel* was no good as I'm not pregnant. Then read Section 13, *Our right to cancel*. Says a membership will be terminated if "your conduct puts our employees or members at risk."

At that moment, *Pumping Iron* and *Sparkles* combined to provide my escape plan. Will do it soon.

Can't believe Flexy likes Max. He's fake as *Adidas* four-stripes.

THU 20 AUG

Was on a bench, mid-workout, glancing around in a daze. Everyone follows everyone here. *Sparkles* is a sheep pen. People copy routines, exercises, even what days they train. But it's the people who copy clothes who annoy me the most. Some male Fit-Fish types wear spandex shorts *over* spandex tights. The ones online look like *Ken* dolls. And just like Ken I bet they never get it on with *Barbie*. If they sold Ken today he'd come with a man-bag and mirror.

FRI 21 AUG

Train delts even though it wasn't delt day. Did so many sets of side raises I lost count. I like going nuts on Fridays. Pulled t-shirt sleeves up to peek in the mirror again. They're so good it creates a problem. People will assume I look like that all over. Bet that's what Max thought. He was doing dumbbell bench and when he finished, he sat up, looked into the mirror and saw me. He was in shock. Then Flexy-Lexy walked by going in to her room. I said "Hi Lexy" because I was high on deltoid dopamine. She did a mini wave. I turned to see if it got a reaction out of Max but there was nothing. Could sense he was still processing my delts. After a bit, Ken picked up his man-bag and probably went home to his mirror.

2 a.m. Distracted by delts and forgot about escape plan.

3 a.m. You want these, Max? In your genetic dreams.

SAT 22 AUG

Otis came in. Looked podgy so I steered our chat towards his job. He said London taxi drivers have a huge hippocampus from learning the streets. The hippocampus remembers things but it forgot to tell Otis to stop eating. He did his body fat and it came out at 34%. He asked "Is that good?" I said adding fat was okay when adding muscle.

He smiled and got three lots of Manager Des's *Triple Threat*. And he paid using coins from his taxi tips which made me feel worse. Said he double-dosed pre-workouts at rush hour to out-earn other cabbies. The police might have to stop drivers for supplement abuse and hold their ears to check for tingling.

SUN 23 AUG

Manager Des threw a newspaper onto the counter at work. He knows I'm born the same day as Bieber so thought it was funny. Bieber's now the face, body, and bulge of *Calvin Klein*. Manager Des said "You could do that!" Then Steve said "In his dreams."

Soon as I got back I slipped into Sunday gloom. Sister's books say you shouldn't focus on what you don't want or you end up getting it. Maybe that's why I ended up seeing Bieber. Then got saved by the planets when I saw a video comparing Bieber to a beast called *LA Zar*. Some weird host asked girls who was more attractive. Normally turn that stuff off, but because of the day's events, I didn't. LA Zar won 6 votes to 5. Worrying that Bieber only lost by 1 vote despite the other guy having an outstanding physique. LA Zar has a ridiculously groomed beard though, and such preening is a female trait. Still better than looking *like* a female so he deserved to beat Bieber. Just.

2 a.m. Dad said "Love yourself, don't wait!" in his sleep and woke me up from mine. He wouldn't beat Bieber.

SUNDAY SUM-UP

You 'mirin' brah?

- ZYZZ

Weight: *10.7 dictionaries* (new PR - closing in on Beaver)

MON 24 AUG

Shouldn't have mocked the mongrel because focusing on him created another run-in. Happened in slow-mo but I reacted in fast forward. Max and goons started using an incline bench next to the newbie they tried to bully before.

The kid had rested some 2.5s against his own bench and was using them for little increases each set. That reminded me of me. Max was wandering around looking for 2.5s as there aren't that many around. I watched him give up and then spot the kid's 2.5s. He assessed the kid, decided he was a non-threat, and casually went to take his plates. I rushed over and asked why he didn't check to see if anyone was using them. He said "What's it got to do with you?" I snatched the plates from his limp grip and delivered the killer blow. Told him "What's bad for the hive is bad for the bee." Mongrel Max froze as philosopher Fox gave him brain freeze! After a long pause, one of his little goons announced he'd found some 2.5s so Max turned away. Handed the kid his plates back. It was a Vin Diesel "FAMILY" moment! Left the gym hyped-up yet determined about leaving.

Got an email from uni with an offer to re-join in September instead of next year. Not sure what to do but dad's still bonkers. One week to decide whether I save my mind, womankind, or my family. It's a lot of pressure. Maybe that's why my shoulders are so good, because I'm meant to carry the world on them.

TUE 25 AUG

Some guy asked to share a bench today. After his set he said he'd seen me train and noticed my improvements. Realized he was the guy who stared before. I panicked about having to invent a girlfriend but he then said something creepier. He works for Fit-Fish. Even showed me a *LinkedIn* page then mistook my relief for excitement. He works in "Talent & Acquisition" and said he's interested in "us" working together. Weird. He asked what was my "social presence" like and it took me ages to decode what that meant. When I shook my head he said being "fresh" was an asset if "handled". The gym was lively so I couldn't take it in. I said I'd be leaving *Sparkles* soon and somehow he got my number. Most Fit-Fish fanboys would have a killer workout after that but I felt awkward and decided to go. As I was leaving he saluted goodbye. Didn't salute him back.

Got home confused so I was relieved to hear something simple. Sister's arranged the annual family trip to the seaside. We're visiting Brighton, the *Jersey Shore* of Britain. Also known as the home of human potatoes.

WED 26 AUG

Spent today rehearsing my escape plan. It's quite scary for a non-confrontational artist like myself. But my destiny, and the destiny of many women, depends on my courage. Felt better when I went in for my session with Flexy-Lexy. Told her I was leaving to help keep an eye on dad. Her sympathy stare combined with stomach-revealing singlet made me feel faint. Seemed like she'd just trained and her abs looked completely flat. She must sleep in the plank position. She can plank over me any time.

THU 27 AUG

It *Sparkles* no more! All it took was barefoot squats. The gullible Max noticed and went off to tell someone. Then manager came over.

Him:	You'll need to put some shoes on.
Me:	What if I don't have any?
Him:	It's unhygienic.
Me:	Are shoes from the street clean?
Him:	Being barefoot is dangerous.
Me:	Can nylon stop a 45-pound plate?
Him:	You've got to put something on.
Me:	Arnold was barefoot in *Pumping Iron*.
Him:	This isn't a movie.
Me:	Not yet.
Him:	What?
Me:	Exactly.
Him:	Look, I'll have to terminate your membership.
Me:	Right.
Him:	Do you understand what I'm saying?
Me:	I own two dictionaries.

I nodded with Oscar-winning sincerity and went to the lockers. Found Max lingering and he scuttled away. He chucked something in the bin which didn't drop because of his clumsiness. Had a look and it was a bottle labeled *RAD-140*. He can't even trash his vitamins and yet thanks to Arnold, I'm now the true *Terminator*.

FRI 28 AUG

Felt great to wake up and not worry about fizzing out at *Sparkles*. Then thought about the uni offer and started fresh worry. I'm still a poet, soon to be a great one, but if I go back now it could be difficult to keep up all my training.

Now I'm free of the bro gym, I need to be free from the content I'm feeding my mind. People like Max make me sick. Influenzas.

SAT 29 AUG

7 a.m.	Sister saying "Up, up, up!" outside my door.
7.30	Woken again. "Get up lazy sausage." Disturbing.
9	On the train to Brighton. Are we nearly there yet?
10.30	Arrived in Brighton.
11	Arrived at guest house. Can't check-in until 2.
11.10	At a café. Could be a café anywhere.
12 p.m.	Eating chips.
12.10	Attacked by carb-loving seagulls stealing chips.
12.30	Walking along seafront.
1.30	Still walking. What's good about the sea? Just a shared bath.
2	*Seaview Guest House* has no sea view. Dad has own room. I'm with sister. What am I, 10?
2.30	Beach. The worse someone looks, the more naked they get.
5	Going for early dinner at spaghetti place.
7	Walking-off spaghetti overdose on pier.
7.20	Punched boxing machine. Sister beat score.
8	Another café. Wrist hurting from punch.
9	In bed. Sister and dad downstairs at the bar.
11.50	Sister came in room and turned all the lights on. She will never get a boyfriend.

SUN 30 AUG

Today was a repeat of yesterday. If this was a movie it would be a montage. I'd be the deep soul watching others play sandcastles on the beach. The deep soul would realize they must make a decision.

3 p.m.	Leaving Brighton. Supposed to be diverse.
	Diverse as *CrossFit*. And not Venice Beach.
3.30	On train. Dad and sister sleeping-off ethanol poisoning.
	Reading her self-help book. Says we must have people who act like advisors when we're uncertain. Says they can even be famous people or dead people. Who is my virtual "collab"?
6 p.m.	Back at the Fox-hole. Separate bedrooms.

Looked up Max's vitamins and they weren't vitamins. They're called "SARMS" for short or *Selective Androgen Receptor Modulator* for long. The make muscles respond better to fuel from the rocket boosters. Apparently not illegal but also not that researched. Articles say they're for cancer but he's too cocky to get ill. Must be to make his fat legs fatter. Some scientists analyzed the sewers under London and found more traces of SARMS than cocaine or ecstasy. Probably came from his house. Anyway, must forget him now.

Six months 'til my birthday. I must make them better than the six before. I must make a better plan and carry it out. I've decided who can help, someone who knows this territory. I'll ask someone who has good brain genetics plus physical proof. I'll ask someone who doesn't flip-flop. From now on, when I'm stuck, I'll ask WWDD? As in, *What Would Dorian Do?* and not *What Would Dad Do?*

Dad excels at doing nothing.

SUNDAY SUM-UP

Find a wise teacher, ask him your questions.
Someone who's seen the truth will guide you on the path to wisdom.

- THE BHAGAVAD GITA

PRO

MON 31 AUG

Asking *WWDD?* worked already. I got Dorian's answer, got dressed, and joined *The Iron Pit*. Almost turned back at the door when I saw the scary looking sign and the fact I'd have to go down some stairs again. Thought I'd do a quiet workout but it was rammed. Serious bodybuilders ignore holidays as their only calendar is their routine.

The owner's called Forest. He wore a baggy sweatshirt but I can tell he trains. If something breaks I won't have to deal with a suit who knows Pilates but not the pec-deck. Forest stashed my cash without counting it. Asked what the heaviest dumbbells were and he said "90s". When I said "Pounds?" he laughed and turned away.

No dad-bods here. These guys don't waste testosterone on babies. No rules on the wall either, just pictures of bodybuilders. In *Sparkles* they had staff pictures. There's still loud music but no prancing. Couldn't see any pre-workouts but spotted coffee and jacket potatoes. This place is a man's kingdom and I'll get built by osmosis.

Got back and watched *Makaveli Motivation* videos. Was so psyched-up I took my top off and almost tore through the house but then heard sister come home.

Today's a tipping point. Even got a funny story about Bieber. The companies who did his ad campaign admitted they enhanced his bulges. All of them! How embarrassing. Beaver and me are now half a year older but only I'm wiser. And my bulges are real.

Almost forgot Hugo's birthday but sent a text. He replied fast and said he was with Seema in a country hotel. I did a witty reply but the message didn't deliver. Must be the poor signal where they are.

I knew Bieber was hiding something. Should change his name to *Justin Sider*.

TUE 1 SEP

Woke up to an email from uni. Hadn't replied in time and now can't re-join until next year. Sort of don't care.

Almost left for *The Iron Pit* then Flexy called. Voicemail said the manager won't allow me back in for my remaining physio sessions. He's still broken from my barefoot beatdown. Then she said there could be an alternative and it would "Be good to see you." Would it? Absence makes the physio's heart grow fonder. My back's better but I can't let a hot chick go to waste.

Was thinking whether I should start recording my workouts in a training log. Asked *WWDD?* Then watched some videos and Dorian's a diary keeper! He's got every single workout from 1983 to 1997 written down. Fourteen years of sets, reps, weight and diet, plus anything that might have affected his training.

Got to the gym hyped and tried out more equipment but left without writing anything. It wasn't even the lack of breast-feeding. It was overheating. Didn't want to look too small so I wore two sweatshirts. Even before the gym thing I've used double-layers to get double-respect. Will wear one from now.

2 a.m. What about 1½ layers? Yes. I'll wear my vest.

WED 2 SEP

Sister's persuaded dad to work. She gave him a pep talk on Brighton beach and now he's going to seal envelopes at home. Embarrassing Fox family antics. She says it's a logical transition to employment. Assuming he transitions to licking 30,000 envelopes each week. 30,000! Even going Monday to Sunday, it means doing 10 a minute for the whole day. Not my kind of reps. It's basically child labour. Suppose that's what you get for watching cartoons.

THU 3 SEP

Watched some *More Curls, More Girls*. Kreed wore a white vest again and looked how I wanted to look at Bodypower. The topic was about testosterone levels dropping in guys getting ready for competitions.

Felt my levels rise when I realized we have a blessing for boulders. Delts could be my only gift (apart from words).

Not sure you can win a show with just one body part, not that I'd ever do one. Not sure you can win a girl with just one body part. I'd be happy to ever do one.

FRI 4 SEP

First day benching in *The Iron Pit* almost became my last. Started smooth and then I bumped it up. Got two, but on the third rep the bar became an elephant. It was too near the neck to roll it and didn't have the air to shout. Had flashbacks of almost crushing the rocket. Just when I thought I'd never get close to a woman's groin, one straddled over my face. A deep voice said "I've got you" and racked it. I sat up and went pink. Pink as her pink leggings. It was a woman in an all-male gym. After the double shock I thanked her and checked to see if anyone noticed. Thought she said her name was "Arnie" then realized it had to be Annie. Sort of recognized her but could be the lack of oxygen. She had a twinkle in her eye so I might have taken her breath away also.

2 a.m. I know who she is. She brushed by going into the Dorian seminar. Well, she went in and I didn't. Wonder if she realizes? Hope not. No one could forget her though. Looks like a tanned muscular pirate with jet-black hair and fake pecs. *Annie-Bolic.*

SAT 5 SEP

Quiet morning at work so went into the equipment area and tried the *Yates Row*. Steve walked past sipping coffee and laughed. You don't grow lats from laughing, dough boy. Think I got the technique but couldn't bend over much as it could create a rainbow risk.

Went to the gym and Annie was at the counter when I walked in. The hyper-lycra-loony hugged me and said "What we training then?" Her hug cut-off my IQ and we ended up doing back together. Mentioned the Yates Row and it turns out she mastered it at the *Temple Gym* seminar. She kept walking behind me during my sets and saying "Legs". What have legs got to do with lats? Then she asked if I could feel my lats working properly as it can take time. Told her "Yep. Better *lat* than never!" She didn't smile.

SUN 6 SEP

Went to the gym after work again. It was a ghost town but didn't give me the Sunday feeling. The gym is a force-field from the outside world and all its troubles. Had a great time trying stuff out.

Walked into the changing rooms after and they were also empty. Decided on a progress check. Could tell the mirrors didn't have a fault like *Nemo*. Took it all off (but kept my vest on) and found the light just as a guy came in. He held his hands up as if to say *carry on*. Pretended I was done and got changed. Saw him swap his shirt. No white vest, just black muscle and a silver chain. Only saw his back but was impressed. Not being gay, but what does the front look like?

Got chatting and his name's York. He helps out at the gym. Reckon he's about 50, dad's age, but that's where the similarity ends. When we shook hands I noticed his triceps wobble. If I shook dad's hand he would wobble. Only been here a week and know a gym friend and a non-family female. I think she's female.

SUNDAY SUM-UP

If you don't look that big, then you don't look that big.

- DORIAN YATES

Weight: *10.8 dictionaries* (osmosis working)

MON 7 SEP

Someone banged on our front door at 7 a.m. and I went to answer. It was a driver with a crate of cardboard boxes. Was in dad's name so shouted upstairs but got no reply. Why is everyone asleep when it's a crisis? Had to bring it in myself. Did last box as sister and dad descended. She assumed it was more rabbit food and said I was "taking the gym" too far. When she realized it was stuff for the child slave, both slave and slave master disappeared.

Went to the gym angry but the universe was waiting with open metal arms. *The Iron Pit* has a pullover! It was hidden in the corner and didn't see it before because it doesn't even have a weight stack. Have to add plates to it. It's made by *Nautilus*, the brand Dorian uses. Did tons of sets. Such a strange but solid feeling. Unloaded the plates and headed out. York thanked me for putting my weights back. If only he knew I lived in cardboard city.

TUE 8 SEP

Got a voicemail from Fit-Fish man asking if I'd thought more about our chat. He hoped I was "smashing it at *Sparkles*." He said to call when I'm "up for the merch and mark we can offer."

Hate abbreviations in writing but in speech it's worse. These people think I'm a desperate coat hanger for their wet-suits. The Bodypower t-shirt was lame. Sorry guys, been there, done it, got the scuba gear.

WED 9 SEP

The house has turned into a factory. The child slave sits on the factory floor surrounded by cardboard boxes, envelopes, and a bottle of water to keep the saliva going. Apart from licking envelopes he has to stuff each one with a leaflet first. The leaflets change. This batch promotes roof cleaning, the height of sophistication.

As usual he has cartoons playing. Tried to explain the maths of his task but he turned and said "Sssshh. Daddy's here now." Sister heard then showed up and said "Don't be negative". Negative? Did Henry Ford succeed by watching Micky Mouse?

THU 10 SEP

How does a woman get to train in an all-male gym? This was my first thought. Got to the gym and my second thought was why did KK call it "The Iron Spit" when no one spits? And no one drops weights or bullies. And in *Sparkles* someone wrote "Your mother..." jokes on the toilet wall plus numbers of girls with descriptions of naughtiness. Toilet graffiti here is different. Thought someone was talking to me with "YOU GOT NO TRAPS MATE" while a possible reply to it said "YOU GOT PALUMBOISM". The last one sounds medical. There was also lady's name on the wall but without bragging promises of what she'd do. No nonsense, just name and telephone. She's called *Diana Bol*.

FRI 11 SEP

Looked up *Palumboism*. Sort of medical. Dave Palumbo was a big 90s bodybuilder who on a few big occasions had a big gut. Someone in the fiendish forum added *-ism* to Mr Palumbo's name to describe anyone with a big gut. Most bodybuilders today have big guts. People say it's caused by *Growth Hormone* or "GH". I watched an interview where Dorian said he took some but stopped it because he noticed no difference. I also read that GH makes soft tissues grow. This means if Bieber's people had acted fast they could have avoided photo-faking his bulges. It also means if Dorian gave it up he must be confident about all his body parts.

2 a.m. "Diana Bol" is not a woman's name.

SAT 12 SEP
1992 - DORIAN YATES WINS THE FIRST OF SIX MR OLYMPIA TITLES

Steve mocked almost every customer today. Soon as they left he muttered "Gear-head." *Gear* is a very British term for steroids and Americans prefer "PEDs" or *Performing Enhancing Drugs*. I noticed the customers he mocks always look better than him, never worse. It's like he's saying *if I can't look like that naturally, then nor can you*. It's like a spoiled little girl stamping her feet in denial. Most debates about whether someone's "natty or not" go that way. But though most do cheat, maybe a few don't. Maybe they're freaks of nature.

We accept other freaks. I mean no one accuses a giant or dwarf of being fake. And I've never heard anyone say my freak intellect is fake. There seem to be three types of chemical status:

- *Nattys* - those who haven't done drugs
- *Not nattys* - those who take drugs
- *Fake nattys* - those who say they take nothing, but do

It's only the fakes who deserve disrespect. If you don't take drugs, okay cool. If you do take drugs, okay cool. But take drugs and pretend you don't, not okay, not cool. The take-and-fakes always want to sell something, usually a supplement or a program. Sometimes they sell their ego by saying they really know how to train or pick the right parents. Fake nattys are the true danger.

I said all this to Steve. He laughed and said "Gear-head, gay-boy." Homophobic and musclephobic but works in a bodybuilding store.

SUN 13 SEP

Did another late gym session after work. Store closes at 4 on Sundays and the gym closes at 6. The last hour's golden. Started training and saw York under the Smith Machine repairing it. Walked over and asked what exercises he did for triceps. He said "Same ones you do." We laughed and I went back to training.

Ten minutes later he came over and asked how I did my pushdowns, so I showed him. First he took off the straight bar and swapped it for a single rope. Said one-sided made it "more electric". Did that before until mongrel Max put me off. Then he shifted my body so my arm went outward not forward. Said it aligned the muscle. Finally, he stopped my range of motion shorter. Said full-range can wreck elbows and "pain's no joke." He went back to fixing the Smith Machine and I went back to fixing my form.

Came back to find dad licking and stuffing envelopes. His range of motion was also short but not productive.

SUNDAY SUM-UP

Stimulate, don't annihilate.

- LEE HANEY

MON 14 SEP

Pushed myself up in bed and triceps felt gone! Mr Weider would be happy I've made pain my friend. Spent two hours scrolling around before I got out. Googled lots of training questions and the fiendish forum keeps coming up first. They still have no manners, no grammar, and host many Dunning-Kruger clowns. Tried *Reddit*. They spell better, speak kinder, and have humour. That's important when finding out forearms shouldn't be bigger than calves.

Mother's birthday today. Completely forgot. Like she forgot to breast-feed me. Karma. Tits for tat.

TUE 15 SEP

Noticed that besides coffee and potatoes, Forest hands out brown paper bags. Even saw Annie-Bolic get one. Had a look at the price list behind the counter but couldn't see much that needed a bag. I asked York why Annie's allowed to train in an all-male gym. He said "Just one of the boys, you know." I didn't.

WED 16 SEP

Arrived at gym really late and was rushing. York noticed and said I could stay on after 10 as he was closing-up. Helped him tidy the stray plates and dumbbells but needed his help to rack some 150s. Ended up there until 11 and got a free jacket potato after.

We chatted about workouts and women. He asked if there was a future "Mrs Freddy Fox" and I said it was years away. Then thought about Flexy-Lexy, maybe because it was a Wednesday. I told him we were close. Only a slight lie as she has touched me during physio.

THU 17 SEP

Annie and I both reached for the same dumbbell. She said "My bad" and I said "Mea Culpa." She paused, yanked the dumbbell off the rack, and went. She has a long way to go in achieving the perfect mind-body combo. But won't joke in Latin from now.

I went off to use a barbell and was about to put a collar on when I realized no one uses them. It's not fake macho, it's that everyone knows how to train.

Dad's been warned about his slow slave output. If he misses the target by *one* envelope he doesn't get paid yet the company takes what he's done for free. He doesn't care. If this is how marriage ends up I might stay single.

FRI 18 SEP

York was behind the gym counter today as Forest's off. Finally asked about the brown paper bags. He said "The levellers?" No wonder the membership's so cheap. Forest levels the playing field by selling steroids. Quite impressed that criminals can use metaphors. York said he was surprised I needed to ask. It's not that surprising. The last time I got a brown bag I was 5 and it contained an apple.

SAT 19 SEP

On my way to work I remembered Annie-Bolic getting a brown bag and realized she's literally anabolic. Suppose it was obvious really as I've never seen a girl do pull-ups before plus she doesn't even do them with the CrossFit cheat.

Went to the gym after and thinking about Annie must have attracted her to me. She came over and said she had a proposal. Went pinker than her pink leggings again. She said she wanted us to "do couples" and I went pinker still. She meant *couples bodybuilding*. It's when men and women compete against other men and women in a bodybuilding show. She did one before but her partner "Shredded Steve" had "peaking issues". I didn't ask. I only asked whether we had to be a real couple. She laughed and slapped my back. Then asked her if she thought I was capable. She said I didn't need to be big as that would make her look small. Told me I needed to be "coordinated and hard." I asked her to clarify that *hard* meant *defined* and she laughed and jolted my back again. Told her I needed time to think. She said to take as long as I wanted until tomorrow.

What's the worst that could happen? I get some experience? Girls always bang on about that. It's six weeks today. It's called the *Halloween Freak Fest*.

SUN 20 SEP

Awoke in panic so I asked *What Would Dorian Do?* Found out today's when he retired unbeaten. Wondered if that meant I should retire unbeaten. Not sure about doing something with someone else. My superior mind didn't develop from being a team player.

Couldn't come up with the answer at work either. Went to the gym and spoke to York. He asked what was in it for me and I said experience. He looked confused. Annie came up and York left me stranded. She started with "So?" All I could do was nod. Then she hugged me and said I wouldn't regret it. Sort of regretting it already. Then we swapped numbers. Sort of regretting that also.

Suppose I should embrace my uncomfort zone. Read that in one of sister's books. Getting nearly nude next to a muscular and tanned *Captain Jack Sparrow* will make me uncomfortable.

2 a.m. Captain Jack texted "Couple but not couple!" with a link. It was Lee Priest competing on stage with his mother. What's scary wasn't how good Lee looked at 17 or even how amazing his mother looked aged 40. It was the fact that his mother had a big brachialis.

SUNDAY SUM-UP

The reason I like bodybuilding is because it's all me.

- DORIAN YATES

Weight: *10.9 dictionaries*

MON 21 SEP

Tried out some machines while waiting for Annie to show. Surprised myself by pushing two plates on a chest press. I felt smug then realized it's designed to do that. It's like the Fit-Fish labels. Their men's XL shirt was tiny and I bet that was a trick to make me feel big. Fake sizes, fake machines.

Snapped out of it when I saw Annie's fake chest. She's done our plan for the next 6 weeks and let me keep my weekends free to work.

Monday:	*Legs* (quads - glutes - hams - calves)
Tuesday:	*Pull* (back - biceps)
Wednesday:	*Push* (chest - triceps - delts)
Thursday:	*Legs* (quads - glutes - hams - calves)
Friday:	*Pull* (back - biceps)

Asked why chest was trained once and she said that's all she needs.

TUE 22 SEP

Woke up in a sweat from worried about getting on-stage. Then watched a video which said stage lights are so bright you can't see anyone. If I can't see faces, it can't be like a mirror. In theory I could dance like no one's watching. Or pose.

Hope York doesn't think me and Annie are a real couple. He watches from the counter and smirks. Today's session was no smirking matter. We were on pulldowns and after my set she told me I could have done more. She said "You did 6 last time." Thought she had an amazing memory until I saw her looking at a training log. Not only is she disciplined enough to write down her workouts but she's writing down mine as well. I've now got a muscular teacher who watches me do my homework.

WED 23 SEP

Push day with Annie. On flat bench she stood over my head again to spot me. This time I turned pink because I saw York smirking. Walked past after and he said "I won't tell your Lexy girl!" Why does he always catch my embarrassing moments? Realized I never see him train yet he looks amazing. True penthouse genetics.

2 a.m. How is my Lexy girl? Bet she feels guilty for paid sessions I've not used. Read in sister's book that girls will "yield" if they feel guilty. Sister had scribbled over it. Will text Flexy tomorrow.

THU 24 SEP

Legs with Annie. Even if I was breast-fed I couldn't have counted how many sets we did. My theory about legs being a source of energy is right. After training I was flat. Came home and slumped on the couch. Eventually recharged and did YouTube on the TV. Remembered sister's books mentioning the power of visualization so typed in "fox bodybuilder". Someone called *Bertil Fox* came up. Could tell he was no relation and that's apart from him being black and weighing 7 dictionaries more. He trains like he's a machine in a production line. He's hydraulic. Dad walked by, stopped, then said "He's a Fox." He claims a friend knew him. Bet he's faking interest to keep me on his own production line of licking envelopes.

11 p.m. Zonked with no inhibitions so I texted Flexy. Mixed poet skills and sales tactics from sister's books.

Hi Lexy,

We've got some of your outstanding sessions, outstanding.
Let's finish our unfinished sometime.
Whenever it suits you, of course.

FF.

Who can resist written charm? My pen's a lethal weapon.

FRI 25 SEP

Pull day with Annie and she forced me to do pull-ups. They're the toughest exercise and made tougher by touching. Apart from her always doing more reps than me there was the shame of getting a "butt bump" from her palms on my buttocks. I might welcome such a touch but not in the gym. Must get stronger.

Told York my doubts about the show. I hoped he'd give me advice but he just listened. Freaked me out as most people offer opinions and I'm uncomfortable using my own. And coming up with decisions is like squats for the brain.

Asked what his favorite song was as Annie had mentioned posing. *Higher Ground* by Stevie Wonder. He says it's about reincarnation. I have decided I'm not coming back as me.

2 a.m. How is Flexy-Lexy resisting my written charm?

SAT 26 SEP

10 a.m. Flexy-Lexy unresisty! Said I could have my remaining physios sessions at her place. Her place! That's girl-code for being interested. Expect she can only be herself away from *Sparkles*. Told her I was at work but would see her later. Wang heard and offered me *Horny Goat Weed* pills. He said they "make girl sing". Didn't know what that meant but swallowed two without water.

8 p.m. Already back at the Fox-hole GODDAMNIT! Went to Flexy's flat, sat in her kitchen for five, then she told me to go into another room. It wasn't her bedroom. It was her garage. Sat face down on her therapy table and got a full hour of *Sparkles* gossip. Gotta confuse me as a member, right babe? She only wanted someone to talk to. Or talk at. When I got up my spine was fine but my confidence was totally out of alignment.

2 a.m. Horny Goat Weed making me "sing" as in can't stop wheezing. First Terrible Tribulis and now No Good Goat Weed. Wang Kerr!

SUN 27 SEP

Felt down at work. Terror Turk asked what was wrong so I explained about Flexy. He said where he came from women were "like mountain goat." He smiled like I understood and slapped my back. Why does everyone slap my back? His story telling skills might have been lost in Turkish translation but somehow it helped to think of Flexy as a mountain goat.

Did I give her the wrong vibe, the friendly vibe? Is that what Terror Turk meant about the mountain goat? If the shepherd gets too friendly the goat never respects them. I should have punished her with my shepherd's staff. I think that's what I was planning.

2 a.m. Woke up during a *Spectator ONLY* dream. The hand holds out the ticket and does nothing else. Something's shrinking my manliness and remembered *More Curls, More Girls* saying shows could do that. Looked up hormone boosters. Found *Tongkat Ali*. It means "Ali's walking stick" in Indonesian. Almost a shepherd's staff.

SUNDAY SUM-UP

I don't work out for chicks.
I work out to create an aura.

- ZYZZ

MON 28 SEP

Intense *legs* with Annie. She doesn't believe in rest and I followed her around like Dirk O' Flynn's dog. By the time we finished I wanted to curl up in my kennel. Instead, we stood side by side and flexed legs in the mirror. Hers are bigger. God has a sense of humor giving women big legs and men the opposite. Men with big legs are more female. Men like Max.

Watched *More Curls, More Girls*. He said most natural hormone boosters were nonsense but Tongkat might work and it shouldn't induce "gyno". Found out that meant breasts on a man. Wasn't paranoid until then. Anyway, as he's Canadian and blondish, he's trustworthy, so I ordered 6 bottles of 60 caps under dad's name. Can't have our postman feeling sorry for me as people already think poets are depressed.

TUE 29 SEP

She's mental. It was *pull* and I wasn't up for deadlifts after legs yesterday. Had to borrow wrist straps from York for the final set. Crouched down, tightened up the straps, let out a sigh, and WHACK, Annie slapped me twice across the face. Jumped up to lash out but got yanked down because I was attached to the bar. Almost tore my arms off. She said "Get angry, yes boy." Did six reps.

Finally experienced deadlifts as a whole-body exercise. The blood rushed to my legs, back, and both cheeks.

WED 30 SEP

Rain put me off leaving for the gym so ended up scrolling. Fit-Fish has a new channel called *Fit-Fish Wreck*. Each Wednesday they have a treasure trove of "special" athletes who do very "special" exercises. In reality it's when one clown or two does embarrassing stuff.

Used the anger to get me to the gym. Arrived with soaking feet as trainers battered. Chatted to York as I dried off. Noticed he was in *Adidas* and turns out we both love their stuff. We bonded with a laughy handshake. Told him about my collection. He asked why I wore old ones if I had new stuff. Explained I was saving them for the right time. He said whenever he buys a new pair he laces-up and walks out wearing them. "Nothing like that new shoe feeling." Made me remember when I begged to do that as a kid but wasn't allowed. He patted me on the shoulder, looked at my trainers, and said to be careful I "don't wear out before they do."

Annie texted to say she couldn't make it. Just realized she doesn't worry much about training silicone. Did chest myself and got quality atoms. And it was a pleasure to train without fear of being assaulted.

THU 1 OCT

Two deliveries to the Fox-hole today. First, another truck load of boxes containing envelopes and leaflets for dad.

Loving son brought them in as usual. Was angry about how it would interrupt my gains until the postman showed up with delivery #2, the Tongkat. Ripped it open and downed one without water. Satan's Rocket! Had to sprint to the fridge for orange juice as it was the nastiest, bitterest pill I've ever tasted. If good medicine tastes bad, this must be amazing.

FRI 2 OCT

Dreaded *pull* again because of deadlifts. Annie says they're for back but it's all spine and legs to me. Only kept up by using my old exam trick of *Doritos Chilli Heat Wave* and *Coke*. It's the pre-workout par excellence. I can imagine Chad Showcracker PhD shaking his baseball-capped head. Listen up, Chadders, I know what works for me. There's legitimate pseudoscience behind it. And even if it's the placebo effect, the effect is real, so put that in your Showcracker pipe and smoke it. Feel nothing from the Tongkat though. No wonder Indonesia isn't an economic powerhouse.

2 a.m. Tongkat's affecting my language. It's like gear for my already voracious vocabulary.

SAT 3 OCT
1970 - ARNOLD SCHWARZENEGGER WINS FIRST MR OLYMPIA AFTER TRICKING SERGIO OLIVA INTO LEAVING THE STAGE BEFORE THE POSEDOWN IS OVER

Asked Terror Turk about excess hair removal. Turks are extremely hairy and thus extremely knowledgeable. He said beard trimmers were good so I got one at lunch. Came back and saw an oversized Otis chatting to Steve. Hid in case he wanted to test his body fat. Steve, fat enabler, processed 4 lots of Manager Des's *Triple Threat*. He loves welcoming more chubbers into his bulging tribe. Even heard him tell Otis "Don't bother using those scales."

Got back from work and dad had John around, the friend who apparently knew Bertil Fox. It was actually true. John and Bertil were both drivers on the *London Underground*. Every few months during night time track inspections, engineers found tuna cans in the *Northern Line* tunnels. They couldn't understand why as passenger windows didn't open. Bertil, who was en route to becoming a pro bodybuilder, ate tuna during his shift.

Once he finished eating, he'd stop the train *mid-tunnel*, open the driver's door, and drop the empty can out. The track engineers never solved the mystery, and unless they read this, they never will. Bertil was called "Beef" in his pro career when he should have been "Tuna".

SUN 4 OCT

Stupid family. Tried clippers before everyone got up. Was doing chest when the batteries failed and jammed the clippers on my hair. Then with perfect timing the bell rang, creating a crisis, and as usual all other Foxes were asleep. Put a t-shirt over the clippers and went down. When I opened the door it was two *Jehovah's Witnesses*. They took one look at my mechanical bulge and went. Scissored the clippers free and rushed to work.

How did new batteries go so quick? Maybe they were cheap Chinese batteries? If I'd been Chinese I wouldn't have needed clippers. China's economy thrives as their naturally smooth men don't need to waste time shaving. Also explains Turkey's failure.

Still annoyed about Annie slapping me on Tuesday. Training for a show is painful. If it's not assault and battery it's just batteries.

SUNDAY SUM-UP

There is no reason to be alive if you can't do the deadlift!

- JON PALL SIGMARSSON

Weight: *10.9 dictionaries* (osmosis effect peaked?)

MON 5 OCT

Woke up realizing sister or dad must have used my clippers and drained the batteries. Felt ill thinking about either usages. I look leaner though, a few percentage points drop in body fat, and that's handy as I'm not liking this starvation thing. Diets are female and that can't be good for my manly mind.

Asked Annie about our music. She said I'd choose it. Felt manly until she handed me a shortlist.

2 a.m. Tongkat's kicked in. Dreamt I got Annie back. We were standing in a moonlit gym and she slapped me. She went for a second slap but I caught her hand. I stared without blinking and she dropped to her knees. Then I whipped out the rocket and gave her a face like a painter's radio.

TUE 6 OCT

Dad got a warning about his slow envelopes output. Worried about him sinking lower so I offered to help. Wish I hadn't. Opened the new batch of leaflets. It's a limited-time membership offer for *Sparkles*. How annoying. Even more annoying was when dad started reading out "*Where - - - - - wellness - - - - - never - - - - - sleeps.* That's clever." Feels like I'm helping my son do his homework. Actually, having a son's impossible as I'm still procreation-free.

Helped for 2 hours then went to workout with Annie. Had paper cuts on my fingers which is bad enough but badder when doing back. Why did she pick pull-ups again? When I dropped my reps she dropped her head. She asked if I was losing my "mojo". Remembered last night's dream and definitely had my mojo in that. Started smiling which annoyed her.

Today, dad and me both got warnings. Be watching cartoons next.

WED 7 OCT

Annie was in a good mood because of chest day so I asked what happened with Shredded Steve. He had drunk endless cups of tea during his prep but never counted the spoonfuls of sugar in each one. Epic fail. It got more epic when she brought up a photo of them together on stage. Shredded Steve is Steve I work with! Now I get all his inadequacies. Annie said the *Halloween Freak Fest* is her chance to erase the shame. Got her to send the photo by saying it was reverse motivation.

Bet it's like John Travolta. Sylvester Stallone trained him for the movie *Staying Alive* and forced him into great shape. Then Travolta hated exercise so much he stopped it completely and became fat for life.

Steve is now fat for life.

THU 8 OCT

Draining *legs* day. Did set after set of squats in the power rack. I felt the calcium chip off my spine after set five and then we did five more. My injury from *Sparkles* nagged but I soldiered on. After we finished I told her I picked *Ain't Nobody* for us to pose to. She said I must have "felt the lyrics". I just picked the coolest melody.

Spent the evening flat out on the floor. Thought about something Mr Weider wrote in *Ultimate Bodybuilding*. He said lifting alone is dangerous. Maybe. But it's still safer than lifting with a loony.

FRI 9 OCT

Woke up in so much pain I forgot about the workout. Then heard dad shout "Guy called Andy wants to speak to you. Says he's from the lion's pit." My sleepy thought was "Who do I know in a zoo?" Then I realized the psycho had called me at home. Checked mobile and saw six missed calls. Got dressed fast. A few seconds later dad shouted "Andy says you better call him back." Got to the lion's pit late and she wouldn't speak to me. Hoped I'd missed deadlifts but only missed the warm-ups. Went right into heavy sets and without any food. If I end up like Ronnie Coleman it will be Andy's fault.

SAT 10 OCT

Bought posing trunks at work. Shredded Steve Travolta did the transaction so I said they were for a friend. He laughed. Then he kept commenting about the size. Could have said I knew about him and Annie but I didn't. He's already clogged with sugar and spite.

Lucky a customer took my mind off it by asking for advice. Wanted to know if we had anything to boost "excitement". Told him to sleep well and avoid stress and licorice. He looked sad and walked off. Then I had brainwave. Tongkat's hard to ship so no one bothers. Walked over and said I had a Chinese friend who's selling special herbs to select Westerners. Told him it wouldn't be through *Underground Muscle* but that he could come next week to pick it up. Mr Excited lived up to my name for him and we agreed terms. I was excited also. Only Steve brought the mood down. He kept smiling.

It's only posing trunks. Anyway, like all measurements in life, there's only three sizes. Small, medium, and liar.

SUN 11 OCT

Used fat scales. Said I'm fatter. They are Japanese so it could be a factory fault from a stressed-out worker. Steve saw me upset and added on some new posing-trunk related humour. He kept saying "Yes Freddy Smalls! Yes Freddy Smalls!" Way too early for a Sunday morning so I took my phone out and flashed the photo of him and Annie. Who's laughing now, dough boy? Asked what happened but he wandered away. Wang said "He time of month."

SUNDAY SUM-UP

It's simple. If it jiggles, it's fat.

- ARNOLD SCHWARZENEGGER

MON 12 OCT

Went to see Hugo at his pharmacy job. Said I needed to divide my vitamins and wondered if they had any containers. Mr Patel saw me and gave Hugo a nod. I got 10 brown plastic pill bottles for free.

Arrived at the gym before Annie so I lingered around. York saw me grinning and asked why. Told him about the Tongkat. Annie texted to say she'd be late so I sat with York and watched him eat a jacket potato. Asked if he took supplements but he shook his head. Said most pros don't either. Then said he did take *glutamine* but I shouldn't bother with it as it's only for "old guys". Asked him loads more supplement questions. After he ripped through most I joked that nothing worked. That opened the floodgates on what did. Forest's brown paper bags. York had so much drug knowledge I had to ask the obvious. He said "I haven't *taken* them."

Then the loony showed up and we did legs. Felt easier than normal so even talking about drugs is anabolic. Annie said we're training late tomorrow. Asked York if he knew why but he didn't. He's got a day off which leaves me more exposed. Went home and divided 300 caps of Tongkat into ten 30-cap bottles.

I've become the captain of chemical capitalism, the Musk of money, the Branson of Bulges.

2 a.m. York might be on Dirk's duck eggs or Mud Man's noodles.

TUE 13 OCT

Did *pull* and found out why we were training late. Posing practice. The gym was empty but still glad York wasn't there. Can't believe how painful posing is. It's like trying to break out of handcuffs combined with crushing a can of *Coke*. Tensing the lats is especially hard. It's difficult to contract left and right equally and tensing them causes an out-of-breath feeling.

Should have been more careful with the posing music. Annie said the one I picked has "perfect" points for us to come together, drift apart, and spin. What are we, ice skaters? And it has lyrics about looking into each others eyes and me putting my arms around her.
If I do that the size comparison won't favor me. She asked how my cardio was coming along. What cardio? Did my standard nod and mumble. No one challenges a mumble.

WED 14 OCT
1925 - EUGENE SANDOW DIES AFTER PULLING A CAR OUT OF A DITCH

Trained *push* in the morning then went back at night to bump into York. He didn't take steroids but had worked for a UK mega-supplier. Said they had links worldwide and controlled the business even if others in the business didn't have a clue. Called them "Nexus". Wanted to hear more but Forest needed him.

Got home and had to look it up. Nothing. Only thing I found was what it meant in the dictionary.

Needed something mundane after so I did a test with the razor. Instant definition! Instant size! No wonder Annie's legs look bigger than mine.

2 a.m. Watched Mitch Viola who said cardio was important for fat loss. Kreed said the same. As did Menial Jerks, Boston Barbell and The Other Jeff. Only X-Man said he didn't do it. Says he only cheats on his diet once a year. What if I've cheated 287 times this year? I better stop. I don't want to get slapped again.

THU 15 OCT

I must be in contact with the universe. Saw a video of Viola slapping a guy called *Ray Man* at an expo. Ray Man's got a following and had told them to cause chaos in Viola's videos. It's called an "Order 86". According to *Wikipedia* it's when a chef runs out of a dish or wants to kick a customer out. Ray Man's followers obeyed his request and ruined Viola's comments.

But Ray Man bit off more than he could chew because Viola realized who he was and challenged him to a slap contest. Ray Man agreed and Viola mashed his cheeks twelve times. They were only slaps, but slaps from a 300-pound guy, and Ray Man was shocked. Annie's slaps hurt and she's half a Viola. Viola told Ray Man his Order 86 stuff wasn't cool. Seems both sides were bullies and none of that's cool. The whole episode should be 86'd forever.

FRI 16 OCT

The clipper-shaved hair is growing back fast and my definition's dropping faster. Quite annoyed because now I'll have to cut carbs and add cardio.

Helped dad with envelopes but only did licking and not stuffing as didn't want to get injured before my workout. It's quite relaxing. During it, he doesn't criticize me or talk, and I don't talk or think. It's almost a proper father-son relationship. With cartoons.

SAT 17 OCT

Annie texted while I was at work. She wanted to know about my tan. She's getting sprayed on the day but I'm not keen. Saw videos of it being done and it's too intimate. Bought *Cal-Sun* fake tan from the store and tried a dab at lunch. I've gone yellow from working underground but mixed with the *Cal-Sun* I should go a nice orange. Will need to practice applying it. Still remember the holiday when sister used sun cream to burn "FWEDDY WILLY" onto my back. Had to keep covered-up for the summer.

Left work, got on the tube, and when I got out there was a voicemail. Thought it was Annie but it was Fit-Fish man.

Hate strangers contacting me on a Saturday like they're trying to catch me out. I'll call Tuesday. Can't have weekend cortisol spikes.

SUN 18 OCT

Mr Excited came in. Took him up to the equipment area, grabbed my bag of delight and teased out the Tongkat. He looked excited at the brown bottle and he excitedly paid £30. That's a £20 profit.

Arrived home and jumped in the shower before sister came back from her Sunday run. Noticed her *Veet* hair removal cream. Tried some on my forearm and it worked well. Would she be a beast without this chemical assistance? Would all women? From age 10 they all dye their hair. What else do they lie about? The clippers and razor are a 5% drop in body fat and the cream's even better. No wonder girls love it. Millennial women are too lazy to diet and just hide under baggy stuff or squeeze into Fit-Fish.

Worried about my diet though. I'm hoping the body fat scales are wrong from Otis using them.

SUNDAY SUM-UP

If you don't like what you see in the mirror,
What difference does it make what the scale says?

- VINCE GIRONDA

Weight: *11 dictionaries* (definite PR)

Envelopes licked: *2000*

MON 19 OCT

Draining *legs* with Annie. Got so wiped-out my inhibitions went and I asked York about his old job. Wouldn't speak until Forest left.

He said his employer started in the run-up to the 2008 Olympics. The US government didn't want any drug scandals so they asked the DEA to crack down on the American steroid business. The UK was already a thriving drug hub but when they heard what was happening overseas they worried about it affecting them. So big shots here formed a kind of industry body for gear, *Nexus*.

They had one goal: prevent bad press to prevent tougher regulation. Nexus didn't concern themselves with mainstream sport as WADA, the *World Anti-Doping Authority* was already on it. But Hollywood was a big concern, as was bodybuilding and eventually social media. If any of these groups abused PEDs then got sick, got cocky, or died, it triggered politicians and authorities and that threatened business. Nexus started keeping tabs on anything that could pose a problem. They knew who was selling, who was buying, who was denying. Even top US distributors didn't know they were being watched. York said people in India, Pakistan, Thailand, and China monitored what was being made and where it was heading. They even kept an eye on "garage labs" if they grew too big or supplied someone too big.

Nexus started keeping a register of problematic, high-profile, PED abusers, a kind of FBI's most wanted called "the hush list". These 50 men are shielded from publicly or professionally getting in trouble, but if something bad does happen, Nexus will step it up. First they'll pull press reports. Then if needed, they'll pull lab reports, amend them, or create conditions people were supposedly born with. All this is arranged by a contacts list "to die for", media and medical friends in key positions. York's face then went sour. He said in a few cases, where guys ended up in a psych ward or committed suicide, Nexus planted hints to suggest it was completely unrelated to gear. They'd show a *person* was excessive and *not the drugs* they took. Said that's when he left.

Nexus did cool things down, because since they took control, crime agencies have backed-off. Investigations are rare and only about money laundering, not health-related. York said to this day, the DEA still have no idea that Nexus or their hush lists even exist.

Wish this was on a Sunday. It would definitely make it unboring.

TUE 20 OCT

Finally called Fit-Fish guy. He asked their silly corporate question, what did I love about "our brand?" After last night's chat it seemed petty so I joked that Fit-Fish made fat people skinny. He laughed and said it actually started when the founder wondered how to boost his rocket in clothing. I tried to distract him by saying I was preparing for the *Halloween Freak Fest* but he jumped on it. He said raising my profile could help people "pay attention".

He must not get the difference between a local show and touching Mr Sandow's leaf. He rattled on and said they'd offer me free marketing and free clothes. Marketing I hate and clothes I hate!

Freddy knows that if you get anything "free", *you're* the product. They don't call us Foxes cunning for nothing. Said I'd think about it.

WED 21 OCT

Did early *push* with Annie. She hardly trained because her silicone was still in-shape but I did and really struggled due to low carbs. Have cut down from 400 grams to 100.

Came home, had shake and helped dad as there were envelopes to finish by Halloween. Despite staring at *Sparkles* leaflets I felt a surge of energy. Sister says it's the universe's reward for helping others. Felt good so I went back to the gym to ask York about Hollywood. When I mentioned Mickey Rourke being drug-free, York laughed and said "He doesn't even pretend!" After that I waited around until Forest went again. I had to know.

York said people think stars get special training and diet help, but they don't. It's something Nexus promotes as it distracts from the truth. He said "Ever noticed how *elite* trainers come from nowhere?" I hadn't. They're picked for their media skills not technical skills. Fancy programs, chefs, electrical muscle stimulation, utter nonsense. A person of average intelligence and income has enough resources already. Hollywood differs in one way. The gear. York said they "always, always" use pharma-grade. It's predictable, potent, and safe. And there's only one weapon of choice. It's not *Tren* or *GH* or whatever the fiendish forum types say. It's "ox". That's oxandrolone, also known by the trade name *Anavar*. The Nexus group know what the studios want. Ox is a pill and that avoids common needle problems like usage, storage, and safety. Pills also avoid scars that can be costly to fix with CGI. Unlike other orals, ox is light on the liver, handy for those who also abuse alcohol, sleeping pills and pain meds. It can affect the kidneys and CV system, but they last a long time, and well beyond the main chunk of an actor's career. Plus it leaves the sex drive intact and the movie business doesn't work without that.

Most importantly, ox gets "the look". The big studios want some size but not too much. Hollywood lighting is a magic filter that works best when someone is lean, and ox boosts metabolism.

It also generates huge pumps, a screen actor's last-minute touch-up. It's high anabolic, building enough muscle in a hurry, and low androgenic, keeping gyno, gut, and bloat away from the lens. Dramatic increases in strength are common, which helps prop-up the belief that actors are heavy-lifting, hard-working naturals.

And, if used sensibly, even actresses can handle it. York said Nexus insiders love their poster girl who used it for a famous action sequel. Two years later, her friend did the same in a music biopic.

Ox is sourced direct, with any shortages got via the "ATM". That's AIDS, Turner Syndrome and Muscular Dystrophy. People with these conditions legally get ox to deal with *cachexia*, muscle loss. California has over 100,000 people with HIV and many sell Nexus their meds. Nexus then feeds this lab-quality stock into distribution, making sure that Hollywood never runs dry.

York made zero deceit gestures through all this, plus he's the most sincere person I've met. But what he said is sincerely disappointing.

No wonder I don't look *A-list* yet. Can't even get sister to stop our peanut butter supply from running dry.

THU 22 OCT

Did *legs* on low carbs then went to the supermarket on my way home to pretend I was normal. Got through the store without buying anything but stopped at a food bank by the exit. Some sad person had donated *Doritos* and I picked them up. Was only having a sniff then felt a hand on my wrist. Turned to see a security guard and then other wage slaves. They said I was "stealing from people who need it most." I wasn't stealing, but even if I was, no poor person would have my blood sugar level. It was so low I couldn't find my way with words. They started to take me to the office but Mr Patel was there on a break and intervened. Told them I was a "good boy". He was wearing his pharmacist's coat and looked authoritative. Did they think I was from an institution? Anyway he got me out.

Was so relieved I felt compelled to help dad with his envelopes.

2 a.m. Changed opinion on professions who wear white.

FRI 23 OCT

Noticed that the hair I'd removed with *Veet* is only coming back today. It's decided, I'll use that instead of the razor. Can't use sister's tub so will have to buy some.

My eating habits are making me bonkers. I'm a slave to a self-imposed schedule and a sister-imposed schedule as she controls the kitchen regardless of my athletic needs. Delaying my shakes is like mother withdrawing the breast. She's such a micro manager, the complete opposite of my free-thinking soul. Don't micro the macro.

SAT 24 OCT

Checked abs before work. They're better but watery. My face is getting leaner more than anything else but at least it convinces Annie I'm on track.

And it convinces Steve I'm on track also. When we opened up the store I saw his eyes dart around. Every week his face looks fatter by comparison. Seeing him sweat for a change inspired me. I analyzed our herbs to see if there was a natural diuretic. Found *dandelion*. It's designed for chubs in a hurry. Got some and will test it on Monday.

Then read up on proper diuretics, the chemical kind. They've killed more bodybuilders than steroids ever did. Worst case I found was Mohammed Benaziza, a guy who inspired Dorian.

"Momo" died from apples, kind of. He refused to drink water near to a show and trusted no one with his food. So he made his own apple sauce. That had water, but in combo with the chemicals, it wasn't enough.

Did more envelopes before bed. I used visualization principles from sister's books and imagined I was sending replies to fans. Future fame tastes addictive.

SUN 25 OCT

Mr Excited came in. I freaked as he charged towards me but he actually wanted more Tongkat. And he wanted to collect on Saturday but that's the *Freak Fest*. His pleasure can wait an extra day.

Bought *Veet* on the way home. Ended up buying talc and toothpaste to feel comfortable. Think it worked as the girl scanned without a blink.

Ordered 12 more bottles of Tongkat for £150 including shipping. Street value as 24 brown containers: £720. I'll out-earn dad at this rate. Did more envelopes as felt pity.

SUNDAY SUM-UP

Most of these guys are genetic Volkswagens.
They use drugs to try to make themselves a Ferrari.

- FLEX WHEELER

Body fat: *Not tested*

Envelopes licked: *3000*

MON 26 OCT

She's bonkers. Annie insisted on walking lunges *outside*. It was cold and dumbbells are heavier when they're cold. Forest must be a secret feminist to let her take them out. Every few minutes, and always during my set, we got interrupted by guys entering and leaving the gym. She chatted away, "just one of the boys, you know", while I dodged *Fords*, *Audis* and craters. And she shouted "Deep cuts, Foxy" as if it was inspiring. The only deep cuts I felt were my knees grazing concrete.

Then we went back inside for leg press, leg extensions and leg curls. When she walked up to the adductor I said I was injured. Actually all the bending had injured the stitches of my crotch and I refused to expose the rocket in a cold gym.

Felt grateful to come back to the warm greenhouse and did dad's envelopes to de-stress. Then tried the dandelion diuretic. Useless. Useless as Captain Jack Sparrow shouting during lunges.

TUE 27 OCT

Woke up and looked down. My legs looked softer and realized it was inflammation from Annie's jogger-splitting lunges. Calmed myself down and went by work to find a rescue. Bought *Melissa Officinalis* also known as Lemon Balm.

Then looked for ways to boost my pale skin and got a tip from *Steve Reeves*, the 1950 *Mr Universe*. He said to eat raisins and drink carrot juice. Something about the red iron in raisins mixing with the orange carotene in carrots. Will use them to carb-up and watch the color drain from my competitor's even paler faces.

WED 28 OCT

Decent last *push* workout. Felt a wicked delt pump and sneaked a peek when Annie went for water. She caught me looking and asked to look. Sort of laughed her off until she said "I'll see it all soon." She'd be quite sexy if she wasn't quite threatening.

Today was the last gym day so I could almost relax. Did posing practice in bedroom with headphones to feel the music. What I didn't feel were sister's eyes as she spied behind the door. I spun around for the finalé, right into her sarcastic face and comment. "Definite ballet boy." And she's definitely staying single.

2 a.m. Realized I'll be in underwear next to a woman in underwear but not how I dreamed it. Did dad's envelopes to de-stress.

THU 29 OCT

Tried on trunks. Haven't worn that style since I was 12 and not sure purple's my thing.

Thought it was best to get familiar so I wore them under my joggers to the gym. Felt perverted. Crossed roads carefully as I didn't want to get hit and have paramedics see them.

Met Annie and we did our routine. She gave me last-minute advice then went to get hair extensions. I stayed and did a carb depletion workout. The idea is to wring the muscle sponges out of sugar and water but add back more later. Then they overfill and it makes muscles look rounder.

York chatted while I walked on the treadmill. Couldn't remember much he said. Will do one more depletion walk in the morning then start filling the sponges, assuming I can get in the kitchen. Sister knows I'm doing the show but doesn't acknowledge it. She's learned man-control from mother.

FRI 30 OCT

Walked first thing to carb deplete. Then had:

- 22 x 1 oz boxes of Californian *Sun-Maid* raisins
- 6 x carrots (medium, from China, mushed)

That's 500 grams of raisin carbs and 40 from the carrots, enough to fill up the sponges. Almost gagged on carrot juice and sister smirked so I had to down it like Rocky's eggs.

Went for shower. Did *Veet* test and was impressed how it improved my lower proportions. Then put it on chest. The warm water and carb rush made me forget the time. Supposed to leave it on for 3 minutes but must have let 6 go by. Glanced down and saw blood running into the plug hole. Jumped out and de-steamed the mirror. It burned off chest hair but also skin. I looked like I'd been slashed by *Wolverine*.

Did last batch of envelopes. Dad beat the deadline. Or I did. Mind still racing about tomorrow. Must sleep. Will do Lemon Balm as I still look watery despite most of my liquid being used to lick.

1 a.m. Lemon Balm works. Less waterlogged already.
2 a.m. Bumped into dad by toilet.
4 a.m. Where's all this water coming from?
5 a.m. Released every raisin and carrot.

Envelopes licked: *5000*

Only had four hours actual sleep. Woke up thirsty. Had *Doritos Chilli Wave* and *Coke* to top-up the sponges. Then read *Doritos* label and panicked about the high salt. Hid them in my prep-bag.

Have 10 hours to relax, do some posing, head out. Can't believe it's at my old school. If I'd looked like this back then I wouldn't have needed to become slick with words. Still haven't looked in *Nemo*.

Backstage

6 p.m.   Doing *Sick Abs Fast* towel movements with Annie to pump up. She's really strong. Or am I really weak?

6.30   Annie disappeared wearing headphones. I might have wiped-off some tan as white towel now completely brown.

6.40   Almost had panic attack and considered leaving. Looked around stage curtain and saw bright lights do hide the audience. Better than a mirror. Will stay.

6.50   Annie appeared as I tried push-ups. Ignored my gesture to help me put oil on the bits I couldn't reach. I'm not an octopus. Ate *Doritos* in rage.

Post-show

I'm drowning in smoothness and shame.

We came last. We failed. Or as Annie told me twice, I failed her. We didn't look like Lee Priest and mother. I looked like Lee Priest, the embryo.

Out of four men and four women, I was the smallest. Soon as I saw our competition I knew we were done. The other couples were full-on bodybuilders looking for an easy trophy.

When we stepped on stage I felt myself shake and it wasn't dehydration. Caught Annie's disapproving stare which made me shake more.

I'd put too much *Cal-Sun* on the bits I could reach and accidentally wiped my face with the towel. The dark bits, my abs, looked like they'd been shot with a cannon. And my face looked like a ghost who just realized that.

Ain't Nobody was a crap choice. Half way through our routine the thug fans sung "You - - - - ain't - - - - got - - - - no - - - - body!" Then Annie stormed-off one way and I stumbled the other.

It got worse backstage. Max was there and he saw me. He was gloating over a *1ST PLACE* trophy. Don't know what it was for but it was a win. How can a loser win?

Even my bus ride back was horrible. Some cocky little kids said "Nice skeleton costume." Hid in bedroom and finished the *Doritos*. Tears came out like *Cal-Sun*.

SUN 1 NOV

Almost skipped work. It was quiet which made me worse. Checked body fat scales, 15%. Checked Max's "socials". Promised I wouldn't. He won a physique category. He slapped "Lifetime natural athlete" everywhere. Lifetime sounds a bit much when you're 20 something. And writing "natural" is like writing "I'm modest" on your dating ad. If you are something, you don't protest it. Plus SARMS being legal doesn't make you a natty. It actually just makes you a fake natty. According to his backstage chomp-a-cake pic, it was his birthday. He's a shirtless Scorpio like McConaughey but I don't buy his act.

KK came in, said nothing, bought two carb drinks and slid one over. I bought another two and slid him one. Sold some Tongkat to Mr Excited but I felt no excitement.

Couldn't face Sunday at home so after work I stopped by the gym. Poked my head around door and saw York. Whispered "Annie" and he shook his head. A male avoiding a female in an all-male gym.

Got on the treadmill and chatted with York. Talked about the show. He asked where I could improve and I said by taking gear. Didn't plan on saying it, just came out. But then I couldn't stop thinking about it. York said I didn't need any then asked what was really up. Should have said mother, Max, and Annie but I just shook my head. He said what someone does is a personal choice, but if do go down that route, I should "Get it from the source, not the shill." Couldn't admit *shill* wasn't in my vocabulary.

Got home. *Cal-Sun* prints of shame still lingering. Doubt Max is feeling shame. I hate Sundays.

2 a.m. Shill means *con-man*. Annie is a con-woman. Or man.

SUNDAY SUM-UP

You have to do everything possible to win, no matter what.

- ARNOLD SCHWARZENEGGER

Weight: *10.6 dictionaries*

MON 2 NOV

The torment continues. Dreamt that Annie came up to me in the gym, reached down, and pulled-off my rocket. No scissors or blood, just yanked it off and walked away. Rather have the *Spectator ONLY* dream than waking up and checking to see my bits are still attached. Must be a warning about women. But it's their fault I'm in this mess. If I was breast-fed we would have won. I'm doomed from the womb. Sister was breast-fed and she's sturdy. After she sucked the last drop, mother turned off the taps. She claimed it ruined her side profile. She's obsessed by looks. I'd never be obsessed by looks. And what about my side profile?

Had a deep think about gear. Watched *More Curls, More Girls* as he's like York and all about long-term safety. He says to have certain things in place before contemplating stuff. I've checked them all. My height, brain and boosters have reached full capacity and I feel fine. I just want to feel more than fine. I want to step into a time machine and pick better parents. Looked up unfair advantages in sport and found out Tiger Woods had his vision *laser corrected* to 20/15. What most people can see at 15 yards, Tiger can see at 20. All I want is a level playing field. A level putting green. Why should mongrel Max have one-up on me? And who else has a one-up? Bet I'm minus ten.

I'm not going to lie or sell anything, plus using gear is legal here, so I see no moral issue. Actually, bet my new body would sell to girls.

TUE 3 NOV

Fit-Fish man hassled again. Do they put pre-workout in the company fountains? His voicemail said he saw the show.

Maybe I'm not made for this? Dorian's an action-man Aries and born on the same day as *Lawn Chair Larry*. Larry wanted to be a pilot but unlike Tiger Woods his eyesight was crap.

So one day he filled up 43 balloons with helium and attached them to his lawn chair. Floated up to 16,000 feet, shut down an airport and caused a huge power cut. Eventually he came back to Earth and got arrested but at least he did it. He didn't wait or hesitate or prevaricate. He just did it. But I'm Pisces. We wander. We ponder. We do wait. I'm born the same day as Bieber. He can't even decide whether he's boy or girl.

WED 4 NOV

Was mindlessly licking dad's envelopes and glanced at a new box. CONTAINS MALTODEXTRIN. Why didn't anyone warn me that envelopes use carbs in their glue? Why didn't X-Man have a video about *that* killing my gains? For the final few weeks of my prep I was guzzling THOUSANDS of mini-carb shots. No wonder the diet was easy. No wonder my energy surged. No wonder I felt compelled to help. That was supposed to be the universe rewarding me for kindness. Turns out the universe is crafty when it wants to punish. Everything's got drugs in it. At least give me good stuff.

Thanks dad. Thanks for helping me seal the victory. Lick the competition. Thanks for helping me push the envelope. Joe Rogan would never let his athletic son be so chemically castrated.

11 p.m. Envelopes are my Kryptonite. Never touching them again.
2 a.m. I hate people accusing me of being natural.

THU 5 NOV

6 a.m.   Today's the day we light bonfires.
Today's the day I ignite my potential.
Going to the gym.

6 p.m.   Had a long chat with York who didn't hide his disappointment but said he'd help. He got up and spoke with Forest for ages. Forest kept glancing over. York came back with a brown paper bag. There was no apple inside but 16 mini glass bottles of *Sustanon 250* made by *Aspen Pharma* in Ireland. York said it was fresh, pharma-grade gear. Said he wanted me to "have the best". Thought that was *ox* but he said it didn't fit my personality. When I looked confused he explained some people become neurotic using it. I asked how actors coped and York said they're always like that.

Each glass bottle or "vial" has 250 mg of testosterone. Actually it's 4 types. I couldn't find any in the dictionary.

Proprionate	30 mg
Phenylproprionate	60 mg
Isocaproate	60 mg
Decanoate	100 mg

York said it's like a 4-cheese pizza with each cheese arriving at different times. Sustanon was the first "designer steroid" and came from Europe. When US rivals tested it, they panicked about how potent it was, and banned its import.

York said it's normally used once every three weeks but that's bad. Once a week works better and twice a week should be my limit. He said half doses every few days is ideal but I might not like the pain. He then apologized about the pain of "23-gauge" needles. I had a look and winced. 23-gauge means big.

He gave me a tutorial on how to inject. It's just like darts or archery and there are four main targets: *side delt*, *side thigh*, *glute*, or *high glute*.

11 p.m. I've been natural for 7919 days. Time for a bit of 7920.

Found it hard to inject myself. Even filling the syringe felt like loading a gun. Then got so tense about doing it I jabbed behind my behind and hit nothing. Thought it was a higher warning but calmed down when I remembered Colin Calves telling me God followed bodybuilding. A minute after midnight I hit the target. Screamed so loud but the fireworks drowned me out. Felt angry about the pain. Might be "roid rage" already.

First shot of Sustanon done. First SOS. May it save our souls. Well, mine. Will ask Hugo about needles. Must be something less painful than these. They're not darts or arrows. They're javelins.

FRI 6 NOV
1952 - DAN DUCHAINE BORN, ORIGINAL STEROID GURU

Annoyed that I jabbed after midnight and not before. Looked up to see if the date had any significance. It did. It's when Dan Duchaine was born, the first "steroid guru". He knew everything about drugs and he was a poet like me. When he got jailed for dealing, he wrote the *Underground Steroid Handbook* in his cell. It was the written version of *More Curls, More Girls* and just as generous. Duchaine introduced whey protein, popularized multiple meals, keto for contests, and even pre-workouts. Just realized I hate all of those. And one of his pre-workouts called *Ultimate Orange* was legendary. Apparently it was so good the FDA banned it.

Weighed myself and not any heavier. Have I injected olive oil? Least it's healthy. Saw a video where Mitch Viola has a fridge by his bed and it's full of drugs and *Ben & Jerry's*. As this place is hot from sister's obsession, I will stash my stuff in the fridge.

Hitting the gym on Monday once the "four cheeses" flood in. Will be ready for anything. Even Annie.

SAT 7 NOV

Got angry with a customer who complained the second we opened. I was sarcastic back. Is that another side effect? In the afternoon I went upstairs to the equipment showroom to see if I was any stronger. Terror Turk was there doing bench press so I did a few. Felt good but Terror Turk was still stronger. He's naturally steroidal.

Back at the Fox-hole I went to mix my anti-Chad in kitchen. Sister was there and said she almost had my "fancy pro-biotic but couldn't get the lid off." Didn't pay attention until I realized what she meant. I almost got my sister on *Sustanon*. Took them out of the fridge and stored in garden shed until there's a better solution.

SUN 8 NOV

York came into the store and I persuaded him to do the fat scales. 12% without dieting! Told him he had great genes and he said "Some good, some not." KK came in and bought 3 carb drinks and we drank like it was a bar for bodybuilders. Gave York the money for the gear and bought him a massive tub of glutamine. He said I didn't have to, but kept smiling at it.

Did some reading at home. No need to store gear in a fridge, that's for insulin and GH. Still think it's wise to keep it cool. If it loses potency, I loses potency. Will hang it out the window in a bag. Hopefully it doesn't get pecked by birds and start a species of anabolic pigeons. Their eggs would be stolen by Dirk O' Flynn.

SUNDAY SUM-UP

I don't do this to be healthy. I do this to get big muscles.

- MARKUS RUHL

MON 9 NOV

First day in the gym with assistance. Annie was around but we kept apart and I surprised myself by not feeling guilty. If that's because of the drugs it's the best side effect no one talks about. People pleaser? Just take gear. Realized that without her I can do what I want so I'm doing a new routine. Keeping the same four days a week though.

Upper body (Monday & Thursday)

Dumbbell bench press	2 x 6
Pec-deck	2 x 6
Nautilus pullover	2 x 6
Medium front pulldown	2 x 6
One-arm dumbbell row	2 x 6
Lying side lateral	1 x 6 (delts already dominant)
Hammer curl	2 x 6
Lying dumbbell extension	2 x 6

Lower body (Tuesday & Friday)

Hack squat	2 x 6
Leg extension	2 x 6
Seated leg curl	2 x 6
Standing calf raise	2 x 10
Back extension	2 x 20
Swiss ball crunch	2 x 20

Texted Hugo about needles. Meeting tomorrow.

2 a.m. Do I really need 3 lat exercises? Just like the idea of people respecting me from behind.

TUE 10 NOV

Met Hugo in *McDonald's*. Brown paper bags again. He emptied out his food and filled it with stuff from his rucksack then passed it under the table. It was 20 much thinner needles. He said they're for diabetic kids but they'll work for anything if used slowly. I thanked him then asked how someone who works in a pharmacy could eat so much junk food. Through a mouthful of fries he said "If it all goes wrong, there's always a pill to fix it." Hugo might be high on love.

An old, crazy black guy was also high, dancing by the counter. He shouted "I'm viral! I'm viral!" but just like all the V.I.P TRAINERS, no staff intervened. I'll only go viral if I don't wash my hands.

WED 11 NOV

Was looking up the influence of genes in sport. It's not just bodybuilding where it matters. Since 1960, Kenyans have won 40% of all the top distance running medals. What's scary is they all come from one tribe, the *Kalenjin*. That's serious penthouse genetics.

After watching Phil Heath plod along during the end credits of *Generation Iron*, I can confirm he's not from that tribe.

THU 12 NOV

York asked my reasons for taking gear today. Why didn't he ask a week ago? Couldn't answer anyway and he gave me quite a look. Then he started putting up a poster on the gym wall. It's for another local show in December, the *Christmas Classic*. He said it might be worth having a go. I questioned why he changed his mind from discouraging to encouraging me. He said he never discouraged me but thinks it's smart to have a focus. He said a focus creates a place to stop and guys who don't have one might get stopped by the grave.

Came home and did SOS #2 with thinner javelins. Much better. Think it's given new life to the old rocket. Shame there's no place to focus that.

FRI 13 NOV

I'm doing the *Christmas Classic*. I asked *What Would Dorian Do?* then watched some videos. Spotted a thread running through his career and everything had purpose. That's why he was successful. York's right, I need a focus. So I signed-up and got one. The entire show is "classic" class, but no height or weight stuff, just experience. Open, Intermediate, and Novice. I'm doing novice even though today I clanged two plates a side onto the hack squat.

Be good to see what I can do when I'm not part of a doomed couple. The winner gets a sword. If I win it, I'll slice off my shame.

2 a.m. Wally Reels warms-up with two plates a side on bench press. Hasn't got my delts though.

3 a.m. When I win it. When I win it. When I win it. Will I win it?

SAT 14 NOV

Arrived at work and kept quiet about the show. Fat people are especially jealous when their blood sugar's low. KK came in and I told him. He bought two zero-carb drinks and slid one over. We clinked no-carbs and he said "Powodzenia" which is something positive in Polish. Was so quiet that Wang sent me home early.

Couldn't face dad's cartoon analysis so stopped by the gym. Walked in and heard Forest say to York "That's a lot of candles to blow out, mate." Asked York and he admitted it was his birthday. I did a lame "I'll be back" impression and rushed home.

Got in, scanned around my bedroom, and saw the answer. Took a deep breath and picked one.

Rushed back to the gym powered by the gear York got me and burst in like a cowboy. Had to wait ages until he was alone then presented him with a *G-Shock B5000D* full-metal watch. He was the G in shock. And then I was in more of a shock as he ripped open the perfectly pristine box and put it straight on. Not being gay, but the stainless steel band looked good on his black wrist. Told him it would match his silver chain which did feel gay but he smiled and shook my hand. Told him it was guaranteed fully water resistant to 200 metres. He said "So you know black men sink!" York must have spectated at swimming lessons like me. Explained all the other features and he listened patiently then said "Time is the ultimate gift."

Made me smile knowing there's another muscular poet in the world. Had an amazing workout. Didn't look at my own watch once.

SUN 15 NOV

Woke up obsessed about focus and Sunday is everyone's least focused day. But realized I can't be like everyone, I can't be like Sundays. Realized I must improve massively. Asked *What Would Dorian Do?* The answer was to find examples of others making big improvements between shows. And ironically he was the best example. Between the 1992 and 1993 Mr Olympia he made the biggest leaps in the history of bodybuilding. When I saw the famous Kevin Horton photos I didn't think Dorian Yates, I thought Dorian Yikes. He put on 17 pounds of muscle between shows. 17!

In interviews he estimated it was "just" 7 pounds of new muscle and 10 retained from not over-training or over-dieting. I reckon he was being modest. If the pics were published fresh today every YouTuber would scramble to do a story. They're the best *before* and *after* photos ever and still get him respect now. Arnold's the public's bodybuilder but Dorian's the bodybuilder's bodybuilder.

Got dressed and went to work. Steve started his jokes early so I shouted "SHOW THEM DIESEL!" and he scuttled away. Focus Freddy has entered the chat.

1 a.m. Looked up 1993 Dorian photoshoot pics again. Printed them out and stuck them on the fridge.

2 a.m. Took pics off the fridge. Came upstairs, taped them to mirror, covered with *Nemo*.

SUNDAY SUM-UP

Knowing when to stop, you can avoid any danger.

- THE TAO TE CHING

Weight: *11.3 dictionaries* (0.7 dictionaries more than two weeks ago! Will overtake Dorian at this rate)

MON 16 NOV

Asked York about GH today and he said it was risky and overrated. Told him I read it makes soft tissues grow. He leaned in and said "You want bigger feet? You want to buy new *Adidas* every month?" Then asked about the stuff Max had, *RAD-140*. York said to keep away from all SARMS even if they're legal. He said *DARPA*, part of the US military, tested them for their *Panacea* program but found too much interpersonal variability, as in unpredictability. In some people, side effects were relatively tame, but in others they were sudden, serious, and strange. He said the military wanted them to be good as they're always interested in an edge, but what they found disturbed them. Wouldn't be specific other than say it was much worse for younger recruits. Said they banned them while most organizations didn't.

Did SOS #3 when I got back and felt relieved it was one part of my life that was predictable in a good way.

TUE 17 NOV

Today was the first time my warm-up on the empty hack squat felt too light and the gravity-defeating confidence got me quality atoms. Spotted Annie watching by the mirrors. Seeing me train legs must be like me seeing a girl wash a car in a bikini.

Got home with my confidence rocketing and an urge to release the rocket. Decided to Rocky-resist and watched videos on those who abstain. They call it "no fap". After hearing their arguments I arrived at a different conclusion. So I wrote a poem about it.

The Philosophy of Fap - by Freddy Fox

> No fap, no fun,
> No fap, no life,
> I'd still fap,
> If I had a wife.

WED 18 NOV

Got angry with sister as we both fought for kitchen space. She said I was being dumb so I reminded her about my 170 IQ and she shouted "IT WAS 107 YOU MORON!" She obviously got that wrong. Being a bigger man than her I did calm myself down and so did she. But then she recommended a new yoga class she's doing. "Because it's yoga on Wednesdays, we all call it *Woga*." At that point her abuse of language brought back my anger and I walked out.

Went up to my room, stepped on a USB stick and screamed. Bet she heard me and claimed a win. Why is she always off when I'm off? Wednesday's called *Hump Day* in America. Now I know why.

2 a.m. Feeling guilty about argument. Is it from secretly using gear? But doesn't she secretly use performance enhancing *Veet* cream? Don't care about hiding stuff from dad. He used me to secretly enhance his envelope performance.

3 a.m. An IQ of 107 would still be above average. She doesn't realize it takes someone of 170 to notice that.

THU 19 NOV

SOS #4. Painful injection this time. Think my buttocks are becoming a dart board and if the dart lands where it's landed before it hits the pain bullseye. Tried the other side but don't have the co-ordination. Mother's fault as the lack of breast-feeding has stunted my hand-buttock dexterity. Feels terrible to realize this on *International Men's Day*. Can't sit around moaning though. Mainly because it hurts to sit.

FRI 20 NOV

Couldn't sleep last night as every time I turned, my buttocks hurt. Dragged myself to the gym. Asked Forest for a pre-workout but he only had coffee. Then he smiled and offered "plant-based energy" pills. Needed energy and with no *Doritos* around I took three. Then he made me a coffee and cut open a grapefruit. Said to eat half including the bitter bits. Thought he was mad but people seem persuasive when I'm tired. He said "Sit for 20, just you wait." So I did wait but still couldn't sit. Sure enough after 20 minutes I felt a surge of alertness and this time it wasn't envelopes. Started to train lower body and it was a joke. Kept adding weight to *every* exercise. Not quality atoms, but MAD ATOMS. York saw me and joked "What else are you on?" So I told him. He walked over to Forest and pointed his finger at him.

   After double my normal workout I went home and played some *Grand Theft Auto V* to expend more energy. Then cleaned my room and organized dad's boxes. Eventually got into bed but nothing happened. It felt like I'd just woken up. Must be like being Aries.

SAT 21 NOV

Got into work and my energy crashed. Had to go upstairs and lie down on the benches. Texted York to find out what Forest gave me. It was *ephedrine* which is "plant-based" but it's no bloody broccoli. It's what Dan Duchaine put in the FDA-banned *Ultimate Orange*. It's a close cousin of *methamphetamine*. No wonder I went from brazen to breaking bad. Apparently the coffee was for caffeine, which then boosts ephedrine, and the grapefruit boosts the caffeine. York signed-off his text with "Don't mess with it again."

My lack of oomph made me feel emotional and I worried about crying in front of Steve but just made it. Got home and went to bed at 7. I'd gone from Pisces to Aries and back to Pisces within 24 hours. I was Paries.

SUN 22 NOV
1926 - ARTHUR JONES BORN, FATHER OF HIGH-INTENSITY TRAINING

Sold so many bottles of Tongkat today. Not being gay, but gay guys are rampant rabbits. If they made kids the population would double. Ordered one last batch and will leave it at that for a while. Must focus on the show instead of being a mafia boss.

Felt tough until I watched videos on Arthur Jones, the man who inspired Dorian. Apart from inventing *Nautilus* machines, he flew jumbo jets, saved elephants, kept crocodiles, and married six times. In every interview I saw, he dominated the host. If he was around today he'd eat snowflakes for breakfast. He didn't just take the red pill, he downed the bottle. I find his motto "Younger women, faster planes, more crocodiles" a bit difficult to live up to.

SUNDAY SUM-UP

If you like an exercise, chances are you're doing it wrong.

- ARTHUR JONES

MON 23 NOV

Woke up wondering whether a shot *just before* the workout would supercharge me. As I sat thinking my buttocks ached which made me recall what York said about the other places to pin. Decided to test both ideas at once by doing SOS #5 before training and in the new spot. The V.G. ("ventro glute") is v.g. What wasn't very good was my walk home from the gym.

Strolling back I saw a *Domino's* driver sitting on his motorbike. Felt an urge to drag him off it and drive away. Had to keep talking myself out of it until he went. Unsure if it was the gear, the GTA, or my subconscious thinking the guy was Max. Calmed down once I realized I could only drive on screen.

Got in, ordered *Domino's*. Tipped double.

TUE 24 NOV

The brown paper bag of tricks is kicking-in where I didn't expect it. According to the fiendish forum, *Sustanon 250* has a rocket-raising rep. York must have assumed Flexy-Lexy was my outlet but I currently just wrestle the bald-headed champ.

My nipples have the mildest tingling but they're still the optimal 8¼" apart and are sub-1" in diameter. Women have the opposite proportions so I say the smaller the nipples the more manly the man. The only man I've seen with smaller is Bruce Lee and he was a beast.

2 a.m. Looked up how Bruce Lee died. No mention of nipples.

WED 25 NOV

Watched *The Kentucky Kid* talk about bodybuilders leaving the US to train in the Middle East. It's a kind of gains drain. He called them "the camel crew" but not sure what porn's got to do with it. Anyway like most people who go on holiday, people go there and come back bigger. Except it's not fat bigger. It's gaining muscle in spaces that were fully booked. The gyms seem cool but that can't be their secret. Whatever it is, when people pose over there they look especially freaky. *Kentucky* calls it a "magic mirror" which means the lighting's good and the mirror isn't faulty like the one *Nemo* covers.

Got me inspired so I visited the electrical store window again. Hadn't been since April and was shocked at how I looked. So was the member of staff staring. He looked away in fear. I finally found out what it's like to be on the other side of panic.

THU 26 NOV

Did SOS #6 after the gym to avoid threatening *Domino's* drivers. Only problem was my co-ordination goes wonky in the evening. What would it be like to have a girl stick it in me? Should really concentrate on doing it the other way round.

FRI 27 NOV
1940 - BRUCE LEE BORN

Bruce Lee's birthday.

Not being gay, but he looked amazing in a white vest. According to reports, Bruce Lee died from a bad reaction to a headache pill. Got to the gym and asked York if he thought that was true. York said it was likely and that sometimes, painkillers kill. Told me that in the 90s some British bodybuilders starting taking one called *Nubain*. The Brits took tons because of the heavy training style. He said some took it for legit reasons but soon got hooked on how it made them feel. A few did 8 injections a day and it destroyed their organs. If I did 8 jabs a day I'd die from not being able to sit.

Watched Bruce Lee in *Fist of Fury*. Hard to believe someone can look so healthy then just drop at 32. If that can happen then maybe someone could look unhealthy and live for ages? Can't take the thought of Steve continuing to insult me after I'm dead.

SAT 28 NOV

Otis came in for supplies and a body fat reading. Was desperate for Wang or Steve to do it but they were with customers. My mouth dropped when I saw 49%. Changed the batteries twice but then one reading briefly said 50%. I didn't charge him as paying to find out you're half blubber felt wrong. He bought nothing then wandered out in a zig-zag. Felt sad for a sec and then felt relief. He hadn't asked me "Is that good?"

SUN 29 NOV

Otis is an omen, a warning about being slapdash with diet. Decided I must take my own food and anti-Chad shakes into work instead of grabbing random stuff. It's a month to go and though I'm not trying to touch Mr Sandow's leaf, I don't want to touch rock bottom either. And it would be nice to finally win something. At school, only the nasty boys won trophies. I bought a trophy for myself once but could only afford a girl with a hockey stick. Ended up giving it to sister. That's why she's cocky.

Took a cooler bag in and filled it with three anti-Chads, a peanut butter sandwich, and some pistachios. It's tedious weighing stuff, preparing stuff and carrying stuff. It's even tedious eating stuff.

Don't know how long I can keep it up. Steve watched me at lunch and laughed. Keep laughing, dough boy. Laugh all the way to the 49% club.

SUNDAY SUM-UP

If it's like breathing to you, you'll find a way to get it done.

- TOM PLATZ

Weight: *11.5 dictionaries* (but not going to 49% club)

MON 30 NOV

Got to the middle of the dumbbell rack's second row today. But more than getting strong or even getting bigger, it's the non-bodybuilding effects I'm noticing. I took Tongkat again yesterday and it boosted the already-boosted boosters. Think it made me text Flexy to arrange another session.

Did SOS #7 in the evening and re-sent my text to Flexy. There are three "therapy" sessions left. That's three chances to win me over. I didn't text that.

TUE 1 DEC

Went for a think-walk to focus and saw a temporary road sign which said DIVERSION ENDS. Kept walking for a bit then went back and carried it home. Don't think anyone saw. Tuesday's the best day to commit crime. Put it in my room for inspiration. There can be no diversions until the *Christmas Classic* sword is in my hands.

Flexy-Lexy finally texty. Visiting her place tomorrow. Good old Wednesdays.

WED 2 DEC

Panicked all night about stealing the sign and it started a diversion of constant worry.

Saw Flexy at hers, a repeat of the last session, although she asked if my pain could be from the "psoas" muscle. Didn't have pain but did the universal escape whenever I don't understand. Said "Maybe."

Looked up *psoas*. It's a muscle with a hugely exciting location. Will tell her it's a growing problem.

2 a.m. Even the meaning of psoas is exciting: *of the loins*.

THU 3 DEC

SOS #8. Halfway through my sixteen shots and look more than halfway decent. Was tempted to check my progress in the gym's mirrors but didn't. Unlike *Sparkles*, guys here cover up with sweatshirts and t-shirts, proper double-layers. Asked York about it. He said they love the actual training more than how it makes them look. Then he said most people are the opposite today, they want the result and don't care about the journey. Reckons that's why gear use is booming. He said back in the day, guys talked more about training than drugs, and that included the guys *on* drugs.

York then smiled and said it was time for me to show him the results of my training. Panicked and said I was a shadow like Dorian, only revealing myself on stage. York said Dorian was a pro and that made sense for him but it might not be the way for me.

I reckon York's read one of sister's books. One minute he's all about living "in the now" and then he says I should think about my future. Older people often get confused.

I'm going to start living in the past. I know where I am with that.

FRI 4 DEC

Had a better chat with York today. Asked who his favourite bodybuilders were and he said it was hard to pick one. So I said pick two. He said "Yates and Platz." Then I asked for two he *disliked*. "Wheeler and Oliva." Had to highlight the fact that Dorian and Tom were white while Flex and Sergio were black. Plus Oliva touched Mr Sandow's leaf 3 times but Tom didn't. York said he hadn't noticed. Was about to ask more but Forest called him.

Either York's developed self-hatred and joined the Klan or he's rainbow-friendly and likes blond muscle men? I'm not blond or black so I should be fine. I do have muscle though.

SAT 5 DEC

Walked into work and Steve looked anxious. Remember him panicking before. He sees me getting in shape and his pea-brain computes that as him sliding back. Weird how men notice men more than they notice women. I never notice men.

Stopped by the gym after to ask York more about his favorite and least favorite physiques. He disliked Sergio and Flex because they "wasted the dice" which I think meant the genes they got dealt. He liked Tom and "DY" because they "worked with the throw". Sounded dramatic so I asked who his favorite physique was in a pure visual sense and said to choose two again. He smiled and said "I only need one. Me." Got to admire the confidence.

I'm confident that I'm #2.

SUN 6 DEC

Wang was weird at work. About 3 he started waffling on about China's success being due to "careful preparation". Then said I should go to the gym. Told him it was an off-day but he grabbed a low-carb drink from the fridge, put it in my hand, and slapped my back. Normally get annoyed when people slap my back but the drink pacified me. So I went to the gym earlier than I've ever been and it was busy.

Was trying random machines when I felt a tap on my shoulder. The last person to do that was the idiot VIP TRAINER at *Sparkles*. But this was a guy who wanted a spot. We walked from my side of the gym right over to the other side and I noticed plenty of others he could have asked. And so it finally happened, I got singled out to give someone a spot. Felt honored and hyper but managed to focus. There was no "All you" although I almost said "Show them Diesel!" in my excitement. Instead I gave him just enough under-elbow assistance, not too much, not too little. A Goldilocks spot. I was so connected with the movement it was like I was training. He said "That was tough. Cheers, mate." It may be from a man, but I'm officially sought-after.

SUNDAY SUM-UP

I'm in the muscle. I am the muscle.

- DORIAN YATES

MON 7 DEC

Reached the end of the dumbbell rack's second row. Felt smug apart from the twinge in my spine when putting the dumbbells back.

Saw York engrossed in his phone and had to see why. A garden! Says he finds green stuff calming. He saw me smiling and shook his head. Told me the more chilled out I was the more I could attack the weights or anything. "Calm equals fierce" apparently. Then he asked what I looked at and I happened to have *TikTok* up. He looked through it for a bit then said "Is it called *TikTok* because the people on it have a clock that's ticking too fast?"

Did SOS #9 after while staring at our garden for natural enhancement of the unnatural enhancement. Calculated I've done 2250 milligrams of testosterone in 30 days. A normal man would make 210 milligrams in 30 days. I'm over ten times more manly. Of course I was manly even before gear. Or gardens.

TUE 8 DEC
FEAST OF THE IMMACULATE CONCEPTION

Today people have a meal to celebrate Jesus's mother being a virgin. No one celebrates my status with a meal. Apparently, religious Mary was pure and blameless, unlike my Mary, mother Mary Fox (M.F). When she got with dad, William Terrence Fox (W.T.F) and produced me, nothing immaculate happened. With a M.F. and W.T.F. it's a miracle I'm so eloquent.

Of course sister lives up to her initials and doesn't give A.F.

WED 9 DEC

Decided to look up the old enemy. Max now has 30,000 followers. This time it's not his lame videos drawing them in, it's his physique. He's on something, and maybe much more than the SARMS stuff. Bet he realized all his leg training made his upper half look puny. I understand that but don't understand why he still dares to plaster "Lifetime drug-free" everywhere. It's blatant.

I feel there are three levels of fake natty and he's up to level 2. There's fake, there's faker, and no ****ing way.

THU 10 DEC

Did SOS #10 in the morning to get it off my mind. The threat of doing them at night has been giving me all-day anxiety and affects my workout. Went to the gym relaxed and had garden wallpaper on my phone for more of York's *calm equals fierce* idea.

Was in the middle of hack squats and got thinking about Flexy. Anything leg-related triggers her. Between sets I texted to arrange our penultimate session. She said it was difficult because she's in the middle of moving and surrounded by cardboard boxes. Almost left it there but the mention of cardboard got me thinking. I asked if she could "come to mine", and she agreed, the power of guilt strikes again! This Sunday. Sister's out for ages and dad will be into his cartoons by the time I return. The time *we* return. I'm very excited. I'm very excited for Flexy.

2 a.m. Disturbed at my recent increase in cursing. Might be the gear's fault but must stop it regardless. It's what Chad Showcracker PhD would do to seem cool while actually being a geek.

FRI 11 DEC

York asked how I was feeling today and gave me advice about eating. Told him this was the healthiest I've ever looked. He said people's outsides weren't always like their insides.

Had a look at *The Kentucky Kid* after and York's right. Kentucky covered so many surprise bodybuilder deaths that it almost wasn't news. Most people in the comments ranted about how stupid the dead guy was. It's weird. Nattys often talk about "roid rage" yet I've never seen it. But the thing I see always, no one talks about. Natty rage.

SAT 12 DEC

Wang Kerr! Got to work and saw Steve smiling so I asked what was wrong. Wang sending us off early last week had nothing to do with being generous and the only Chinese success was him having a lady visit the store. Steve reckons he used the benches upstairs which means I won't touch them now.

Wang likes a Brazilian girl but his parents disapprove so he took matters into his own hands. Or hers. They met on the non-Tender app. He smiled all day and considering it was last week, that's some *Pumping Iron* peak-moment. When we closed he took off the yellow *Underground Muscle* shirt and put on another yellow one. Didn't get why then realized it was a *Brazil* football shirt. Wang said "I score before and I score again." I've not even made the team. But must remember to stay positive. Where there's a Wang, there's a way.

SUN 13 DEC

Wang inspired me so much that I started thinking about Flexy's home visit the second I got up. Tidied my room, sprayed sister's yoga scent, and positioned the *Bhagavad Gita* to show I'm cultured.

7 p.m. Got back from work in time to stop Flexy ringing the bell. Quietly got her upstairs into my room then went to make some tea. Started face-down on her chair then she asked me to turn around. She prodded her fist around my hip. Slender fingers. Then got me to open my leg outward, exposing mission control. Wasn't ready for such passion and it took thoughts of Dick Dastardly to delay launch. Luckily she wanted another cup of tea so off I went.

When I got back my door was open and Flexy was talking with SISTER. "Funny how we've got the same name" "It's the best class!" "Woga!" "Yes, Max is very flexible." "We should swap numbers!" While I'd been making tea - and not love - sister came in, bounded upstairs and went into my room. She's always doing that. It turns out even she knows mongrel Max because of the stupid *Woga*. One minute everything was looking up and the next it crashed. And why the hell does Max do yoga in an all-female class? Another gender-bender Annie in an all-male gym. I hate Sundays.

SUNDAY SUM-UP

Why this timidity at a time of crisis? It is unworthy of a noble mind. Do not give in to it. Stand up now, like a man!

- THE BHAGAVAD GITA

Weight: *11.7 dictionaries*

MON 14 DEC

Today's SOS #11 instantly fueled angry thoughts about yesterday. Every time I have a fantasy someone steps on it.

Got to the gym and even York was weird. He asked why I started training. Should have said Bieber but instead told him about the book on ancients and recited a quote from *Mr Socrates*. "It's sad for a man to grow old without seeing the strength of which his body is capable." York said he had a different take. "It's sad for a man to see the strength of his body, without being capable of growing old." He's definitely been watching Kai Greene.

2 a.m. I know what York's doing, reminding me about purpose. Wish he hadn't. I'm no closer to girls than I was 10 months ago. What a Fox-up.

TUE 15 DEC

Finally did hack squats with 3 plates aside, and despite the pain, it made legs enjoyable. My quads are good, my hamstrings so-so. My calves are still walnuts in a hosepipe. Luckily no one judges walnuts. Getting strong has made me realize supplements aren't that effective, especially in comparison to gear. It will be hard selling them now. Must be karma for not honestly answering Otis's "Is that good?"

Got home and realized I need posing music. Even though I'm not a couple, I don't want lyrics that can be weaponized against me. And it must be a simple routine to cope with un-breast-fed co-ordination.

2 a.m. Checked Sumo Fair's channel again. Still no calves either. We could start *Team All-Walnuts*.

WED 16 DEC

Days off from the gym are hard without gear and even harder with it. Got so bored and anxious I did SOS #12. If I do one more by Sunday it I would have done 3 in a week. York said never go above two. After doing the shot I had a mini-panic wondering what I'll do when I run out. Watched a movie to relax and saw *Limitless*. Bad choice.

The guy finds brain-enhancing pills and they really work. Problem is, his stash runs down to zero and he can't function without them. In true Hollywood style and using the last bit of his enhanced mind, he gets a new supply made, wins the girl, and lives happily ever after. Not sure I can do any of that.

At least I've chosen my music, *Forest Gate Funk* by *Zinc*. It's unknown but that's good as most people go for clichés. And most music is better than the body it's supposed to show-off, which means the audience loves the wrong thing.

Better get my actual routine sorted. Can't do it here. Even with a chair against the door it feels like I'm being watched. Mind you, not being gay, I'd watch me.

THU 17 DEC

I'm moving to Alaska. Went to the park at 11. That's the quietest time, no walkers, no weirdos, no mothers. Found a spot off the paths, put headphones in, and practiced routine. It was going well until I came eye-to-eye with Annie. She was carrying her gym bag and smoking. Didn't care about the smoke as much as her presence polluting my mind. She saw and looked the other way which is the most insulting thing one lifter can do to another. I stopped posing. She induced stage-fright again. In a park.

Got back and saw a Christmas card from Fox mother. It had a sad looking snowman on the front and the inside was even sadder.

MERRY CHRISTMAS FROM YOUR MOTHER & SIN!

The irony must be lost on her.

FRI 18 DEC

Did SOS #13 first thing, third shot of the week, and instantly knew it was a mistake. Made me way too edgy. Looked online for a reference of my madness. My week's total adds up to 750 milligrams. Calmed down a bit when I read Mitch Viola could shoot 5000 milligrams. And there's some *3CC* guy who's done 12,000 milligrams. They must walk around wanting to kill people or procreate with them. Maybe both. Maybe in that order. Even if I don't feel good I am starting to look it.

Read that Arnold once took thousands of photos in a short period then released them slowly over decades to look like he hadn't changed, a Dorian Gray move. Texted *Tom's Tripod*.

Went to the gym and got snappy with York. He only asked how it was going but I got paranoid thinking he knew I'd done 3 shots. Can't remember what I said but it was rude. Apologized then decided it was best to leave. Went home and looked at competition pics from the 70s when everyone was "classic". Had a look at one of York's least favorites, Sergio Oliva, and noticed a pre-*Photoshop* secret: his head was the size of a dried pea. His arms looked higher than Arnold's, and maybe they were, but his shrunken skull really helped. Arnold had a melon. And Marcus Ruhl ruled with a raisin.

SAT 19 DEC

Went for a skull-shrinking haircut before work. Was the first one in but midway through I heard a familiar voice. Mongrel Max was in the chair next to me and he saw me look so I shut my eyes for the rest of the cut. After the guy finished he held up a mirror but I didn't look. Felt better as I walked out when Tom of *Tom's Tripod* texted and said it would be a "delight" to help with my photos.

Then rushed to work and Steve immediately made comments about my hair, "Hope you didn't pay for that?" He can't be original. And his hair's only bushy to divert focus from his gut.

SUN 20 DEC

A friend of Mr Excited came in for Tongkat and had endless questions. Answered them and we did the deal. An hour later he came back with even more questions. He ignored the fact I was busy so I said "Take them or take off." Could tell he was a Soho media darling who didn't like my challenge. Also noticed him stare at my upper chest. You only get that with hard training so people recognize it and back-away. Want to intimidate me? Beta luck next time.

Ten minutes later the sprinklers went off and stayed on for ages. Thought it was the universe telling me to cool down but actually Steve had smoked a joint in the staff area. Carpets were ruined but agreed with Wang to not tell Manager Des what caused it.

Feet got soaked and had to take shoes off. Doubly worse as heels had no cushioning from diet. Now I know why office slaves stay fat.

2 a.m. Carbs, carbs, everywhere, and not a gram to eat.

SUNDAY SUM-UP

I feel for food more than I could crave a woman.

- KAI GREENE

MON 21 DEC

Was posing at home when I thought what's the point if no girl sees me? Don't think there will be any hot chicks at the show. Then realized my negativity could be low-carb catastrophizing.

Went to the gym and York wasn't there. Got paranoid he was avoiding me after I was rude but Forest said he'd planned a day off. Wandered around and started a final touch-up workout but stopped. Wasn't happening. Sad atoms. Came home and watched posing videos. Trying to find something simple that works for me. I can't pose like Dorian because I'm not Dorian and doing Arnold's routine is off the menu as he didn't have my delts.

Did SOS #14 before bed. Should have jabbed it in the rocket as that's gone into hibernation.

TUE 22 DEC

Started the day with a stop-start shower and three separate razors to become smooth. Was the most complicated shower I've ever had. I feel sorry for those non-binary types.

Went to the gym feeling like someone else was inside my joggers. Saw York. He looked tired and said it was "ending the year pressures." Knew exactly what he meant. Walked on the treadmill and York noticed me hobbling. Explained to him about my super lean feet. He looked at my battered trainers and asked why I still wasn't in my new ones. I just shrugged and he just shook his head. He jokingly went to lift my sweatshirt to see my abs and I almost fell off the treadmill. Said he'd have to wait. He smiled, squeezed my shoulder, and walked off.

Went home and read sister's book on sleep as I've been struggling. Said the secret was to only associate the bedroom with sleep and sex. That didn't help.

WED 23 DEC

Panicked at breakfast when I hit the bottom of my last *Quad Power* tub. Then realized with a few days to go it wouldn't make a difference. Thought about how Dorian improved his Olympia shape by being relaxed so I started my carb-up a day early. Grabbed his photos from behind *Nemo* and went to see Tom of *Tom's Tripod*.

Arrived and gave him the photos. He disappeared for 5 minutes and came back grinning. He said they "raised the bar" in what we'd achieve. Tom's a pro, a detail man, and asked if I'd shaved correctly. He even had spare razors ready and offered to do the awkward bits. Even Annie wouldn't do that. Was just going to do torso pics but Tom said the lower half told the body's "true story". Anyway the photos looked alright. Only glanced as didn't want to seem vain. Asked if he could convert them into black and white. He smiled and said he wished more young men had my "brutish, bellipotent, bohemianism." Couldn't understand on low carbs but it sounded good. He offered to show me his portfolio and told me he's "done a few pros" but I had to go and practice my posing. Asked if he'd come to the show and get some stage shots. He said seeing me at the end of his long lens would be "pure pleasure".

THU 24 DEC
CHRISTMAS EVE / CHRISTMAS CLASSIC

8 a.m. Saved yesterday's shot, SOS #15, for today. Remembered when the school nurse jabbed my shoulder and it swelled. Realized it might hurt but thought about Mr Weider's *make pain your friend* principle. Split the dose and injected half a friend into each delt.

10 a.m. Already good shoulders looking even gooder.

5 p.m. Checked-in. Saw the competitor list. Max is doing it, exact same class. His full name is *Christopher Aaron Maximilian Power*. No wonder he uses Max. Two other competitors. Tall black guy who's more *Masai* warrior than classic. Needs 2 dictionaries extra muscle.

And a Chinese dude with huge calves but nothing else. Shouldn't have relied on uncle's towel-based workouts.

Can't believe how decent I look. Not doing a proper hard workout for ages has let me fill out. The show's only between me and the mongrel. On in 5.

6 p.m. Shaking.   I WON!!!!! I BEAT MAX!!!!! FOX YEAH!!!!!

I'm covered in fake tan and true glory. Posing went brilliantly. Before the posedown I asked *What Would Dorian Do?* The answer, stand my ground. I let Max, the Masai, and Calves-Only follow me around like Dirk O' Flynn's dog. The bright lights meant I couldn't see but I heard Terror Turk's grammatically incorrect "Kill them dead!" Shame there was no overall title. Not saying I was the best in the whole show but I was in the top 1.

Briefly met Tom and saw stage pics. Max was bottom heavy, the Masai looked like he was from *National Geographic* and the Chinese dude was a dumpling. I really would pick me. I was shoulders and head above the rest. In the poker game of penthouse genetics, it's great to be dealt delts.

Weighed myself at home. Did it quickly as was almost toppling but think it was 11.8 dictionaries. Think that's 1.2 more than the *Freak Fest* and just shy of Dorian's '92 to '93 improvement.

Texted York to say I won and he said "But how did you do?" Must be merry already. He said to come over tomorrow. Said he'll do me a carb-up with extra roast potatoes. Is this a dagger I see before me? No, it's the Christmas Classic sword. And it's mine, Max, all mine.

2 a.m. Dorian's '93 shape was slightly less cherub than me.

FRI 25 DEC
CHRISTMAS DAY

Felt so good waking up today. Hasn't happened since I was 10½. Missed Christmas dinner and raided the fridge then returned to my bedroom for a champion's feast. Told everyone I needed to rest. Soon as I shut my door I couldn't stop eating. Two big bags of *Doritos*, two jars of salsa dip, one big bottle of *Coke*. I may turn diabetic. Don't care. It's just nice to eat without a calculator.

Tom sent me links to all his photos from the shoot and also from the show. One of them even has Max looking down. It's fantastic.

York texted to ask what time I'd be over but told him I was injured. Half-true as feeling tired from the carbs and couldn't be bothered. Will look better tomorrow anyway. Emailed him one of Tom's pics. Wait until he sees me in the flesh. He'll be shocked.

2 a.m. Just realized how far I've come. I used to be a think-tank and now I'm a tank. I'm indestructible.

~~SAT 26 DEC~~
~~BOXING DAY~~

SUN 27 DEC

York is dead.

~~SUNDAY SUM-UP~~

MON 28 DEC

Went to York's Saturday morning. Ambulance. Front door open. Walked in. Police asked who I was and took me aside. Neighbor heard thump Christmas Day. Did nothing. Called around next day. No answer. Called 999. Non-responsive. Gone.

Paramedics said ID chain and condition suggested heart attack. Neighbors are old, and York's family live overseas now, so I've been asked to visit a coroner's office tomorrow.

Can't take this in. Wondering when.

TUE 29 DEC

Went to coroner and signed many forms. Then dread. Prepped me on what I was to see. Led into room and saw York mid-chest up. Thought there's never been a better specimen in the building. Looked so healthy. Ate so healthy. Asked around but they all repeated it was likely heart-related. Was he on gear? They're getting the family's permission to do more tests.

I was judging his physique. Supposed to be the other way around.

WED 30 DEC

Haven't told dad or sister but think they can tell something's up. Been replaying stuff to find clues. Can't remember last thing I said. Just remember not showing abs.

THU 31 DEC

Thought about going to the gym to see if Forest knew anything but couldn't. Realized Annie might know something but couldn't do that either. Will wait and see.

Wanted to do my final SOS #16 before midnight and start the new year clean. Was shaky and dropped the needle. Then it didn't go in and had to jab harder. Then couldn't get it out. Sent me into a panic but took deep breaths and wiggled it free. Looked at my phone and it was 00:01. I've technically taken drugs in the new year.

Didn't do anything else. Didn't send or read texts or chat to anyone, not even sister or dad. Felt like deleting all my fitness stuff. Is there a button to delete real history?

HALF-NATTY

FRI 1 JAN

Woke up worried about stopping gear then felt guilt for not thinking about York first. Then everything merged into panic because I thought he'd plan my next move. Suddenly hit me that I might not have thought this all through. Worry, guilt and panic, the new year's breakfast of champions.

Had to distract myself in the evening and went online but only looked at car stuff. Thanks to *Donut Media* I just wanted to eat donuts and do donuts in a car I don't have.

Should have gone out but didn't want to see all the happy-clappys wandering like stuff's great due to the date change. Least I know I'm a true Iron Pit trainee now as I no longer care about the calendar.

SAT 2 JAN

Was relieved to go to work and more relieved to find out KK had told everyone what happened. Manager Des said I could go home plus take tomorrow off. Agreed to tomorrow off but said I'd finish today. Wang gave me a nod and Steve a friendly punch in the arm. Almost went down like *Slam Man*. Made him happy.

Spent the evening watching some boxing. A few videos later the algorithm decided if I watch shirtless men in a ring I must like shirtless men in a gym. Sister distracted by getting a curry delivered and we ate together. Haven't done that for years. Then we watched *The Shawshank Redemption*. Decent film but Morgan Freeman's character reminded me of an older York. And not sure I can escape what's just happened.

SUN 3 JAN

Shouldn't have agreed the day off. The Sunday dread normally hits evening time but felt it creeping up by midday. Went online again.

Went straight to finding out about stopping gear suddenly. Asked *What Would Dorian Do?* and it turns out he stopped and did nothing. After his last Olympia, he came-off all drugs overnight, chemical cold turkey. Apart from dealing with retirement, he had to deal with a break-up, and losing someone close. Don't know how he survived. Although he didn't give any advice I still got an answer.

He hinted that knowledge was limited back then and if he had a choice he might do things differently. Have I got a choice?

Read more stuff. Everyone talks about PCT or *post-cycle therapy*. Not one person covered post-cycle guilt. Doubt there's a pill for that.

2 a.m. Went to the toilet and washed hands. Accidentally killed a tiny fly by the sink. Tried to save it. Guilt on top of guilt.

SUNDAY SUM-UP

If you want to be whole, let yourself be partial.

- THE TAO TE CHING

Weight: *12.2 dictionaries*

MON 4 JAN

Fit-Fish man called and I told him it wasn't a good time but he went on and said he watched the show. Politely as possible said I didn't want their brightly-colored clothes. Then he asked if I cared about the color "green". Didn't know that meant money until he explained. Why do these Fake-Fish pretend they're American? I stayed silent and he said it's okay to "love the cash" as that's all they care about. And he said if I mention their items at the right intervals they'd do a cash deal for me. Said most signings get clothing. His pushy tone irritated me so I blurted out I'd taken gear. He said "Didn't hear that, and long as no one else does, we're good. Speak soon, buddy."

Re-deleted all my social stuff. This is not the life I subscribed to.

TUE 5 JAN

I'm not the *Christmas Classic* champion. Got a letter from the federation saying I wasn't eligible to compete. Said I'd competed as a couple which is an *open division* and so I shouldn't have been in the *novices*. No one takes couples seriously apart from Annie. They've told me I have to give the sword back. What a Fox-up.

Have sympathy for Lance Armstrong. He gave back 7 swords.

WED 6 JAN

The *Freak Fest* and *Christmas Classic* are unconnected so someone told them. Could only be someone with a motive. Could only be Max. It's always those with something to hide who do the accusing. What are you hiding you double-crossing, sword-swiping thief?

Emailed the federation. They're coming here on Monday. Coming to collect my dignity.

THU 7 JAN

Annie texted. York died of a stroke on Christmas Day, probably in the evening. She said York's sister is here now and asked Forest for my number, and Forest asked Annie.

Looked up *stroke* on *Wikipedia*. Massive list of causes but none made sense. All this health stuff scares me. How do pro bodybuilders do it? Good genes aren't just how your body handles drugs but how your mind handles fear. In *Formula 1* the cars are almost identical and the true difference is braking. Some drivers shut off their fears to brake later and that's what makes them win. Some bodybuilders must be okay pushing themselves into a chemical corner. Some bodybuilders must brake later.

FRI 8 JAN

My rocket boosters have hit the brakes and feel light. Last night in shorts I didn't feel them at all. Before they'd clang like plates but today I felt the rocket swing more. Decided to weigh them. Tried mother's bathroom scales first but they wouldn't register on that. Panicked until I tried a handful of peanuts and they didn't register either. Then went into the kitchen and got my food scales out. Got on tiptoes, rested boosters on scale bowl, used one hand to lift the rocket (didn't want to weigh that) and used other hand to press the button. Did a measurement then went to do another as I'm very precise. With incredible timing dad walked in and I froze. More incredible was him being so zoned-out he didn't notice. As he got ice cream from the fridge he said "Don't weigh your food son, just enjoy it" then left. Felt relieved. Extra relieved it wasn't sister.

SAT 9 JAN

Thought being at work would save me but got a call from York's sister, Dominique. Manager Des let me sit in the office to take it. She said York had *Sickle Cell Disease*. Their parents were carriers which meant a 1-in-4 chance of being born with it. Apart from Dominique, York had two brothers, all fine. York was the 1-in-4.

Went back to *Wikipedia* again and searched causes of stroke. Sickle Cell was buried in there somewhere. Clicked off immediately.

Funeral's Thursday. Store's closed tomorrow while soaked carpets replaced. Sunday dread descending.

SUN 10 JAN

Spent the morning looking at Sickle Cell stuff. Happens when red blood cells get shaped like a sickle, instead of a ball, and then don't flow properly. They cause inflammation, heart attacks, and strokes. There's no treatment other than dialysis and pain management. Read that people end up on that painkiller *Nubain*. No wonder he knew so much. Explains the glutamine too. Does nothing for healthy people, but in those with sickle cell, it dulls the pain.

My muscles are melting like a snowman and York won't even see snow again. What was I waiting for? The only good waiting was the kind he did. Most people with Sickle Cell die by 45. York got to 60.

SUNDAY SUM-UP

Your attitude will take you much further than any genetics.

- TOM PLATZ

MON 11 JAN

Sword collected by an old guy in a navy federation blazer. Neither of us spoke much. I asked if they were certain about their decision and he said he didn't know anything but touched his nose as he said it. Looked that up in sister's body language book. Touching the nose, mouth, or ears is proof of a lie. It doesn't matter now anyway. Liars never prosper. Apart from on social media.

TUE 12 JAN

Feeling the lack of gear. Not just body but mind. Texted Hugo.

Cleared YouTube history but training stuff kept coming up as it's all gone mainstream. That Joe Rogan gets in on everything. He was talking to a Navy Seal who runs non-stop like *Forrest Gump*. Says he overcame terrible things but still has frightened eyes. Watched a few of his own videos and got disturbed when he kept saying "Stay hard." Feels like Special Forces are spying in my bedroom.

2 a.m. Might let Joe Rogan interview me once I'm a famous poet. But only if he stopped using kettlebells. And the *Glock*.

WED 13 JAN

Max put up his social media again and used *Photoshop* to delete me and put the trophy next to him. He also used it to make his legs look more proportionate. For Fox sake. And still claiming natty to his now 40,000 following. Why would you do that?

Not even sure what my own chemical status is. I wouldn't dare call myself a natty now. But I'm free of gear so I'm also not a *not-natty*. And I'll never lie and be a fake natty. I'm inbetween.

I'm a half-natty.

THU 14 JAN

York's funeral. Finally wore some of my rare all-black *Ultraboosts*. Had them boxed since July but didn't care about getting them muddy. I did care about an open coffin.

Freaked me out to look at his face so I went for the hands. He was wearing the *G-Shock*. They played *Higher Ground* as the coffin went into lower ground.

Went to the wake after and saw KK and Terror Turk. It was the most silent I'd heard a group of bodybuilders although there was lots of eating going on. Annie came wearing all-white. York would have smiled. Got chatting by the food table and she said there's another Dorian seminar next month. People from the gym are going up and there's a ticket left for sale. Felt weird talking about it but she was trying to cheer me up. Said I'd think about it and she didn't demand her usual quick answer.

Read funeral card going home and finally got York's full name. *Winston Henry York*. Fitting initials.

FRI 15 JAN

Had a weird realization last night, falling asleep, and thought it again when I woke up. Although it would be nice for a girl to comment on my physique, it would have been nicer for York to do it. Not being gay, but there's stuff only a guy can appreciate, stuff only a guy can say. Haven't trained for ages now and I've shrunk quite a bit. A girl would hear that and say "That's good."

SAT 16 JAN
1993 - JON PALL SIGMARSSON, WORLD'S STRONGEST MAN, DIES DEADLIFTING

Work was quiet. KK came in and didn't say much, just bought his usual two carb drinks and slid one over. Almost bought myself some mood boosters to down with it but decided not to. If my mind got me into this mess my mind can get me out of it.

Hugo's slow so had to look up more hormonal recovery. According to *More Curls, More Girls* I'll need help to fire-up the boosters although sometimes they do it themselves. Two drugs mentioned were *HCG* and *Clomid*. HCG "tells" the boosters to make more testosterone. And Clomid tricks the body into thinking the levels are low, encouraging them to up their game.

All these drugs are chemical motivation, a pep-talk for parts Hugo refuses to reach.

SUN 17 JAN
2013 - LANCE ARMSTRONG TELLS OPRAH HE CHEATED

Another quiet day at work. Terror Turk came in and did a workout. Told Steve to call me if it got busy and watched him train. Watching the shirt-free madman was relaxing, like a late-night YouTube video, nice and mindless.

Got back to the Fox-hole, ate rubbish, watched rubbish. Tomorrow's "Blue Monday", statistically the most depressing day of the year. It's about debt, weather, relationships and regret. Who gets paid to study this nonsense?

SUNDAY SUM-UP

I may be in timeout forever. But I hope not to be.

- LANCE ARMSTRONG

Weight: *12.1 dictionaries* (almost the same as on gear)

MON 18 JAN
1977 - PUMPING IRON RELEASED

The nonsense is real. I just got fired. Someone made a complaint about the Tongkat. Manager Des didn't manage to tell me who it was, but said whoever did told head office, who went ballistic. Idiots. Anyway, no warning, straight out for gross misconduct. The clown who complained is gross. Bet it was the media mongrel. And what was his complaint about? Couldn't please your boyfriend? It's because you're unpleasable.

Came home and watched *Pumping Iron* to cheer myself up. It was released today in 1977. I was released today. Bet no one released Arnold. I'll get a final pay check then I'll have to tell dad. Can already hear him saying "Like father, like son." What a Fox-up.

TUE 19 JAN

I lost my job, my sword, my hormones. I lost my friend.

WED 20 JAN

Fit-Fish man phoned and I picked up wanting a fight. But he took the rage out. He offered me £500 a month for a year plus a £1000 "golden hello" for signing-on. I'd have to set-up social media and post one new clothing item, once a week, for one year. Got off the phone feeling weird. When I went for a think-walk I saw unpaid bills stacked up by the door.

Hugo finally texted. Told him I was worried about the rocket although now I was thinking about the possible need to be in-shape.

Got back from the walk and Hugo texted again to say he couldn't get anything as it's too risky. Then he forwarded details of a junkie ("Waz") who might help. He uses the pharmacy for needles. Dorian's cold turkey route now looks appealing.

THU 21 JAN

This is ridiculous. The rocket won't follow orders. Feel powerless even though I don't look it. Texted Waz to meet Saturday.

Nemo has been over the mirror for almost a year and that's despite me going on stage twice. Why can I look at others but not myself? If I take the Fit-Fish offer I'll be forced to look and it could make me mental. I reckon the constant pressure happens to celebs so it must happen to content creators. The more successful someone gets the more locked-in they become. They've got to stay in shape, stay funny, stay innovative. It's like being at a party you've got fed-up with but your friends won't let you leave. Exhausting.

Considered doing a home workout but thought I wouldn't be able to push. Watched Doctor Doolittle for his thoughts on intensity. The doctor's philosophy was to do it "harder than last time." Can't remember the last time the rocket was harder than a melted marshmallow.

FRI 22 JAN

Was thinking about the Fit-Fish offer then looked to see if anyone in fitness had struggled from pressures. Found two YouTubers. The first was *Murphy's Law*. That law is *if anything can go wrong, it will*. And it did. He started as a guy who took his shirt off in public to shock girls. Then down the line he had a meltdown. Fortunately his camera was running. Within a few weeks he'd achieved enlightenment and re-emerged as a guru. The second one, a strength coach called *Yo Coach!* was a straight-up guy with loads of proper training videos. Then at some point, unlike X-Man, he ran out of ideas and disappeared. But like Murphy's Law, he came back enlightened and his content got strange. Instead of pushing weights and hitting on tyres he ran camps where men pulled-together and stopped hitting on women. His enlightenment revealed them as devils. Not sure what his devil wife thought.

11 p.m. Envelope pushed through door. A 4-pill foil pack with 3 blue pills. Don't know why one was missing but there was a note.

Now you can rise to any occasion! Hugo.
p.s. Good luck with Waz.

You know you've reached rock bottom when your friend helps with your rocket.

SAT 23 JAN

Went to meet Waz in *McDonald's*. Stupid to do Saturday morning as it was crammed with kids. Arrived early and felt suspect so I had to order. Asked for a *Coke* and almost said *Clomid*. Waz turned up looking like his name was short for wasted.

The freak offered weed and *khat*, whatever that is. Declined and went. He stayed to finish my one-sip *Coke*.

If things don't bounce back I won't be able to turn *The Fox Family* into a featured article on *Wikipedia*. Texted Hugo to complain. Cheeky git replied "Things will look up soon" with a winky face. Some stuff just isn't funny.

SUN 24 JAN

One month from the *Christmas Classic* and I've stopped many things. I've stopped gear, I've stopped training, and I've stopped sleeping. The only thing I haven't stopped is the thinking. I even thought about going back to the gym but don't know how I'd explain my reverse transformation. Hypertrophy to lack of trophy to atrophy. Not the greatest conversation to look forward to.

The universe must have heard my fears because I went round to Hugo's and Mr Davenport answered the door. He asked how my "birthday plan" was going. Had to use the *Weider Cheating Principle* and say it was going great. Went up to Hugo's room and even though he was in the middle of getting naked he didn't stop. Realized I've seen Hugo shirtless far too many times, it's almost Matthew McConaughey level.

Told him about York. Turns out Hugo knew of him as he visited the pharmacy for prescriptions. Hugo said he got lots of pain meds but you'd never know by looking or talking to him. That's York.

Then had a chat about Hugo for a change. He doesn't have the overthinking genes I do. He just does stuff. Asked if he wanted his bench back and he said didn't. Asked why he bought it. Said he thought it would help him get girls but realized he could do that without it. Didn't tell me how. That's a Dirk O' Flynn move.

Also asked why there was a blue pill missing from the pack he gave me. Said he tried one with Seema but she said he didn't need it.

Talking about others is bad for my self-esteem.

SUNDAY SUM-UP

I only stopped competing, but I'm not stopping bodybuilding. It's the greatest sport.

- ARNOLD SCHWARZENEGGER

More bills arrived. Fit-Fish could pay them but even as a Pisces I'm not sure about their marine-based brand. They could be sharks.

Burns Night. Impressed that a poet gets his own holiday especially when he only lived to 37. That's modern pro-bodybuilder longevity. I'm 60% of that and not famous. Did the calculations and today's my 8000th day alive.

Hugo texted. He told Seema my problems and apart from the shame she might be able to help. He says she's a pharmacist who likes nature too. She's dropping round *Velvet Bean* and *Kalonji Seed*. Says their combo is an "ancient secret from the village". Hope it helps this village idiot.

TUE 26 JAN

Seema dropped-off the ancient secret in a modern tupperware container with instructions. Mixed 5 grams of velvet bean in water. Tasted of mud. Then chewed 2 grams of kalonji seeds. They made my throat scratchy and the bitterness reminded me of Tongkat. Then realized I still had loads of that unsold. Put two by dad's bed. Seema's my dealer and I'm dad's. He needs it. If he was a *Marvel* character they'd call him *Broken Man*. I'm saving the hormones of a man whose hormones created me. Weird.

WED 27 JAN

Found dad sitting by the computer looking at jobs. He's seen how pathetic his son is and wants to become a normal dad again.

I kept checking LA weather on my phone. You know you're crazy when you check the weather of a place you don't live. I might lack sunshine. *Underground Muscle* deprived me of our planet's battery and now my own battery is at 1%. Sounds like a rival to Mitch Viola.

THU 28 JAN

The battery is charging up. Must be Seema's secret. Clicked on videos with girls in the thumbnail and I'm not even interested in make-up. Poet skills charging-up too, and where there's rhythm, there's rocket.

The Comeback - by Freddy Fox

I used to train, I used to pain,
Slow to start, and then the gain,
I won a show, I won a sword,
Perfect scores, across the board,
And then one day, they took it back,
So Freddy fell, down a crack,
But step-up Earth, save the dreamer,
Mother Nature, great redeemer.

FRI 29 JAN

Got a call from York's sister. Asked if I could lend my support at a solicitor's meeting on Monday. It's a reading of the will. Don't like that sort of thing but maybe I'll inherit another family secret. How to look like you train, without training, would be handy right now.

SAT 30 JAN

Went by the pharmacy and thanked Hugo and Seema for the boost. Tried to downplay the rocket revival and said I'd been missing uni. Seema said it was better to have a gap in my education than a gap in my soul. Almost poetic for a future white-coat.

Got back and saw dad watching TV. He'd swapped *Tom & Jerry* for *Tony Robbins*. Then he asked me questions about Tongkat.

Took a leaf out of his book and changed stuff up. Instead of going online I played a game. Decided the universe, via the dictionary, could predict my future. Shut my eyes, opened a random page, and put my finger on a word. Stumbled on page 449 and got *command*. I felt good. Then checked to see what would have happened if I'd gone 20 pages either way. If I'd swiped right to 469 I could have hit *conclusion* and got depressed again. And if I'd swiped left to 429 I could have landed on *cock*. I think life is safer online.

SUN 31 JAN

With Seema's secret kicking-in I've realized the benefit of low hormones: you don't care about getting laid.

But now I sense the rocket in my pocket and I've got no planet to land it on.

Went back to look at fitness stuff again. Could be a new year thing or being away for a month, but everyone's more obsessed with who's natty and who's not. They were debating a kid called *D Bang*. He didn't look that big but was shredded and strong. Some say caring about who's natty or not is pathetic. If it's to catch people out for fun, it is pretty weak. But sometimes people really want to know what the body can do so drug status is relevant. Don't think people should split into camps. Maybe I'm biased now, but there's got to be good stuff on both sides. Or that could just be me being a Pisces.

2 a.m. Some don't like *D Bang* as his name sounds like cocky code. Like it's for *Definitely Laid*.

3 a.m. Why have I not been laid? Definitely need to.

SUNDAY SUM-UP

Speak your truth, whatever it is.

- DORIAN YATES

Weight: *11.6 dictionaries* (at least hormones are rising)

MON 1 FEB

Dad and me started the day in suits. He actually had a job interview, the power of not watching cartoons. Got to the solicitor's and wished I was back home watching some. When they started reading the will York's sister started crying.

Then they came to me and the solicitor brought up a shoe box from under the long table. Secretary put it in front of me. Had a gift tag on top.

ONLY TIME I DIDN'T WEAR A PAIR INSTANT!
HAPPY CHRISTMAS,
YORK.

Brand new *Adidas Ultra Boost*. Solicitor said to try them on but didn't. Just shut the box and smiled.

Chatted with Dominique after. She said I looked good in the show. Asked how she knew. When she went around to York's place, there was a photo of me, the one I emailed. He'd printed it out.

Got home, put box under bed, fell asleep. Woke up an hour later and found myself training on auto-pilot. During the solicitor's meeting I'd wondered if York knew which workout would be his last. Only did bed-presses and push-ups but they felt good. Felt like a being a beginner again. Imagined York laughing. Laid back on bed and thought about Fit-Fish. Thought if I could be happy dealing with a company that just cares about "green". Or would I prefer to find a different way, to not sell out, to instead just wear what I like. To wear the brand that makes them green with envy, the brand loved by Kobe, Jesse Owens and Muhammad Ali. By York. Wrote email. Unlike pausing uni, my heart didn't beat wrong when I hit *Send*.

TUE 2 FEB

I, Freddy Fox, just put my dad through an arm workout. He begged me. The Tongkat must really do it for him. Was weird to start with, then sort of fun, then annoying. Dumbbell curls went fine but then I was stupid enough to mention their balance with triceps. Anyone who calls lying dumbbell extension "basic" is lying. When dealing with a motor-moron, it's complicated. Was getting irritated then remembered York taking pity on me and I went a bit easier. He annoyed me again so I subscribed to X-Man on the TV's YouTube. The built babysitter can take over.

2 a.m. Disturbed that dad raves about Tongkat so much. Still getting over the time when sister was 5 and walked in on him *naked*. She ran back screaming "Daddy's got a tail, daddy's got a tail!"

WED 3 FEB

Deeply disturbed. Went for a think-walk and stopped in the park to do pull-ups. Wasn't strong but felt good to do lats again. Knew I'd be sore if I didn't eat so rushed home for anti-Chad shake. On the way I remembered running out of *Quad Power* but smiled when I realized I'd stashed away some final scoops of *HustleTech*. Walked in and heard a familiar voice that didn't make sense for the location.

MAX WAS IN MY KITCHEN. Spied from the room next door. Sister and him were chatting and I could see him holding a "Woga" mat in one hand and my shaker in the other. Soon as he left I had a huge argument with sister. Said he'd already caused me problems but she said I had no proof. But I did have dripping proof of her giving him my *HustleTech*. Doesn't she understand the whey's thicker than water concept? She treated an utter stranger like family. Jesus would be disgusted.

The only good thing was when she said he used my food scales and bowl to weigh the powder as he's "very precise". So am I, Max. I weighed my boosters on them last night.

2 a.m. Sent Flexy a pic of Tom Platz's legs. Getting her back for all those times she mentioned the mongrel broflake.

THU 4 FEB

Went for a morning think-walk after reading light helps the boosters. Even wore a t-shirt for the Vitamin D. Saw two girls approach and noticed them smile. Assumed it was at a guy nearby, but it wasn't. It was me. Then he turned to see why *they* smiled. Then the universe smiled because I recognized him. He was one of the nasty boys from school who taunted me with their non-standard use of a towel.

He used to be sporty but now he sports Palumboism. Nice that the girls looked but nothing beats being envied by a bully with a belly.

Flexy replied to my text. *Sparkles* sounds the same. She didn't mention the Tom Platz leg pic. Must think they're mine.

FRI 5 FEB

Another think-walk. Came back in and went into the kitchen to make a drink. Saw the *Mega Mass 2000* I bought for dad's birthday open on the side. Almost expected to see sister or Max with it. Then heard noises. Found dad in front of the TV watching *X-Man* and doing side raises with sister's dumbbells (technically mine). He did a set, saw me, and gave me a hug. He got a job! It's a new place called *Flights of Fancy*. They sell cheap flights. Was just about to tell him that "flight of fancy" means something *imaginative but impractical* but stayed silent as he looked happy. He actually inspired me to go upstairs and do a full-body workout. Who cares if it's for beginners, you've got to love what you love. And whether it's quantity, quality, mad or sad, I love my atoms. Don't love being hugged by dad.

SAT 6 FEB

Watched a short film called *Dennis*. Dennis is a Danish bodybuilder who lives at home with his mother. He tries to get a life and meet girls, but mother always gets in the way. Stopped it there as got uncomfortable. But, not being gay, the sight of big Dennis got me more psyched than yesterday and I finally went to *The Iron Pit*.

Forest was putting up a photo of me on the wall. It was the one I sent York and he said York's sister gave it to him. Looking up at it made me realize him printing it out was a better trophy than a sword. Went home and finished *Dennis* short film.

He meets a girl, parties with her, then she introduces him to her friends and they persuade him to de-shirt. Then random guys turn up and mock him, so Dennis leaves. Finally he goes home, where his mother guilt trips him for going out. Feeling remorse, and like a giant baby, Dennis finishes up sleeping next to his mother. I empathized with the dangers of de-shirting, but getting in bed with my birth vessel, no thanks.

SUN 7 FEB

Overslept as the house was quiet then realized sister was out on her Sunday run. Snuck into her room to grab my dumbbells again but saw her laptop open and took a look. It was a yoga video, paused. Normally ignore hyped-up stretching but the pretty teacher got me to drop my bias when she dropped into *downward facing dog*. Tried a few things and it was relaxing. It became unrelaxing when sister bounded up the stairs. Had to exit without pausing the video.

Heard her go nuts and knew she'd storm into my room so I got on the floor and pretended to be sorting stuff under my bed. I grabbed York's *Adidas* box. She came in, she interrogated, and she left. Decided to then look at the shoes as I was holding them. As I pulled them out of the box, the soles stuck to the tissue paper at the bottom. There was an envelope underneath. Had that word on it.

SUNDAY SUM-UP

Those who know, don't talk.
Those who talk, don't know.

- THE TAO TE CHING

MON 8 FEB
CHINESE NEW YEAR - MONKEY

Chinese New Year. It's year of the monkey and as a human it should be good. Dad's a monkey and started his new job today.

Sister (rat) was at work which made the house feel empty. Then Annie texted to say there's still a ticket for the seminar. It's this Sunday. Not sure I'm up for seeing men on another Valentine's especially as this time they could be more naked than dad.

The envelope I found only has two pages but feel uncomfortable about it. Maybe because it's from York or maybe because of what it says. Hugo came over and that distracted me. After chatting about women and life, it dawned on me that Hugo's a bit like Dorian. Self-confident, philosophical, does his own thing. He does the stuff that sister's books promise without reading any. Plus, Hugo never waits. I couldn't wait for him to leave when I remembered the house was empty as I felt inspired to look up downward facing dog lady.

TUE 9 FEB
PANCAKE DAY

Ate two pancakes and a squeezy tub of maple syrup first thing to get in the right state. Promised I'd never touch another envelope after dad's leaflets but needed to check this out. NEXUS.

It had "the hush list" and a note from York.

NEXUS EYES 50 BAD USERS. POPCORN ARE MOVIE FOLK, COOKIES ARE EVERYONE ELSE. "NICE" ARE UNDER SUSPICION BUT CURRENTLY HAVE NO INFO / CONCLUSIVE EVIDENCE. IF SOMEONE DIES, THEY'RE OFF. IF SOMEONE'S OPEN AND NOT PROFITING, THEY'RE OFF. THOSE WITH LEGIT RX ARE OFF. PRO BB ARE OFF UNLESS THEY DO SOMETHING STUPID. ANYONE ON HUSH IS THERE FOR A REASON. GETS UPDATED.

Then a bit more in pencil that wasn't finished.

SOME ARE STARRED UP.
THESE SPECIAL SIX ARE KNOWN

Wondering if it's the last thing he wrote. What do the stars mean? And don't even know why he's given me it, because I didn't ask. Wish he was here to explain. Actually just wish he was here.

POPCORN	NICE
AK	DC
BA	HJ
BC	JG
BP	JK
CB	JS
CE	
CH	
CJ	
CP	
CT	
DJ*	
EN	
GB	
HC	
JV	
KN	
MJ	
MW*	
RG	
SP	
TH	
TP	
VD*	
WS	
ZE	

COOKIES	NICE
BC	JC
BM	OI
CG	RE
CH	SH
CK	SP
CL	
DL	
GG	
JN	
JP*	
JS	
KH	
KH2	
LA	
LG	
LN	
LP*	
MO*	
MM	
MT	
SC	
SC2	
TL	
UW	
VS	

WED 10 FEB

I realized today that a couple of channels are beacons of harmony. *More Curls, More Girls* isn't natty but encourages safe practices for nattys. And *The Kentucky Kid* who is natty but praises non-nattys. They might not realize, but they're proof that getting along in the fitness world is possible.

What isn't possible is decoding the names. Think I got a quarter. Feel shocked about some.

THU 11 FEB

Went to the gym again. Had another weird workout expecting York to show. Didn't want to go straight home after so I got a jacket potato. Forest came over and asked if I needed to "stock up". Was sitting in the exact place where York had said having a focus meant having a place to stop. Told Forest not for now. He went red in the face for a change.

Walked home shocked at my quick decision. Felt embarrassed at coming across cocky so I came up with other reasons for going back to being bro. Kept hearing seven words, maybe ones inspired by dad. *Doritos were never made to be weighed.*

FRI 12 FEB

Slept so deeply last night, not sure why. Had a dream about Flexy, woke up, went back to sleep and had another about Annie. They're different, but together they have all the qualities of a perfect woman. Wonder if I could get them together?

Went to bed early again but woke up feeling weird after another *Spectator ONLY* dream. Must have been one of those lucid dreams because I forced myself to see more of the hand holding the ticket. First saw the arm. Wasn't mother's. Pulled back a bit further still. Was a reflection. It was my hand. Completely freaked me out of bed.

Put on the light, looked at my two *G-Shock* limiteds and two mint pairs of *Ultraboosts*. Realized it's all keeping me a spectator. Remembered Zyzz selling his *World of Warcraft* account. Listed everything immediately on *eBay* with a really low *Buy It Now* price. Keeping the pair I wore to York's funeral and the ones he got me.

SAT 13 FEB

Woke up to 8 emails, 4 from *eBay* and 4 from *PayPal*. Everything sold as I slept. Just over £600. Could have got more with an auction but don't care. Transferred £100 over to the *Sickle Cell Society*.

Watched *The Program* movie about Lance Armstrong. There's a scene where he takes his shirt off in front of the team doctor. The doc says Lance's shape is wrong for elite-level cycling and that he better try a different sport. Lance proves him wrong and wins the *Tour de France* seven times. I know he was on gear but so was everyone. The doctor reminded me of mother. When she saw me with my shirt off she said I should get myself a new "birthday suit". The doctor was wrong. Maybe she was.

11 p.m. Texted Annie to ask about the seminar ticket. Was still unsold so I bought it. What else am I doing on Valentine's Day? I've probably fancied my body more than any girl has. Don't need a hotel and won't travel back with the gym crew. Sharing a minibus was bad enough at school when the nastiest kid weighed 100 pounds. If the pupils get rowdy at 250 things could get out of hand.

SUN 14 FEB
VALENTINE'S DAY

7 a.m.	Mother texted to ask if I'd stop dad signing the divorce papers. Replied smiley by mistake and didn't correct after.
9 a.m.	Train to Birmingham. Spilled pre-workout. Got 3 coffees.
11 a.m.	Arrived in Birmingham. Had an hour to kill. Wandered into coffee shop. Promised to not get coffee. Got coffee.
12 p.m.	Arrived outside *Temple Gym*. Didn't pause at top of stairs. Needed to release caffeine.

THE GYM

Gym's a group of caves where man first lifted heavy. If *The Iron Pit* is spit and sawdust this is rust and dust. Bizarre mix of equipment. Can tell the boss trains. Spotted *Weider* plates as seen in *Ultimate Bodybuilding*. Nautilus Pullover near the front. The toilets would not score well on *TripAdvisor*.

THE SEMINAR

Must have been 30 crammed in. Spotted Annie, and then Max, who was dressed like a Fit-Fish out of water. Then Dorian arrived, shook a few hands, and it went quiet. Amazing content, stuff not seen or read anywhere.

Dorian gave extra advice on *lats* because people kept asking. Then he asked if someone would de-shirt for a demo. Not one beefed-up guy offered and Max just squirmed. Everyone was frozen and my heart was racing but I couldn't ask Dorian what to do as he was there asking the question. Out of nowhere I asked "What Would York Do?" and then heard him say back to me "Freddy, what would you do?" so I STEPPED FORWARD, I whipped off the shirt and the shame. I did a *Yates Row* corrected by *the* Yates, then pulldowns facing the mirror, watched by Max on one side and Annie on the other. I didn't see myself but I must have looked okay as they looked shocked. Dorian asked how long I'd trained and I said since March 1st, my birthday. He said "Not bad" and THEN SAID if I could get myself out to *Gold's Gym* in a couple of weeks he'd put me through a special birthday session after his seminar!

Had a comedown knowing that won't happen but, not being gay, still the best Valentine's Day I've ever had.

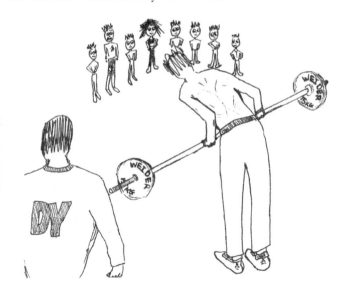

5 p.m. Left the gym and went to a bar with Annie. She started drinking immediately. I had another coffee and apologized for being sweaty as the gym had no showers. She said I could have a "quick one" at her hotel and as I felt hot from the coffee I agreed. Walked back, went up to her room and had it. When I came out the blinds were down and all the lights off. She was sitting on the bed and said "Now the lower body." Almost fainted with fear then remembered what I'd just done, told her to hold on, popped back in the bathroom and popped a Hugo pill. Came back out and it all happened. In the darkness either of us could have been a ripped Bruce Lee but who cares because I'm now NOT A VIRGIN!

Was tempted to re-live the painter's radio dream but noticed the clock and had to rush off. She must have thought I was a total player but actually my return train ticket was only valid for a specific time.

7 p.m. Train back. Text from Sexy-Lexy. Sounded upset, said something bad had happened. Asked me to meet her at *Sparkles*. Kept telling myself *carpe noctem*.

10 p.m. Arrived at *Sparkles*, sign said closed for re-fit. Texted Flexy who appeared and let me in. Crying (her), alcohol fumes, always promising. Downed 2 Hugo pills just in case as first did nothing. Went into her treatment room. Said because the gym was closed for a week she "took the opportunity" to ask Max out for a few drinks. Both got tipsy, she made a move, and he confessed HE'S GAY! Knew the whole face-cloth face-off was suspicious. Why did he wait to confess? No wonder he trained at the pink palace surrounded by women, *The Iron Pit* would be pure porn.

11 p.m. Continued nodding as she repeated the story which was getting really repetitive. Got up to leave then she made a move and I'M NOW A DOUBLE NON-VIRGIN!

It was the best use of her treatment bench ever and the dominance hierarchy got corrected the right way around. Plus I got my final session. The only problem was all three blue pills kicked-in at once and everything looked blue. Felt like I was doing a *Marvel* character especially as she wanted the lights on. She was tearful throughout and kept saying "LEGS, LEGS, LEGS" which threw me but I kept going for the whole 2 minutes. Felt guilty as had just done Annie but felt better when I remembered Flexy encouraged a good warm-up.

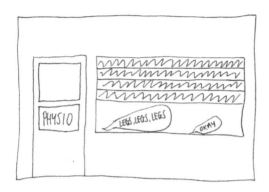

12 a.m. Home. Hyped. Funny how both have a thighs-matter obsession. *Vogue* survey wrong. Should just put up a photo of me.

Today, I ruled like an ancient statue. Today, I became Julius Caesar.

Today - by Freddy Fox

Today I ruled and did not squander,
Today I came, today I saw, today I bonked her.

For the first time in my life, I might like Sundays.

SUNDAY SUM-UP

Know what your duty is and do it without hesitation.

- THE BHAGAVAD GITA

Weight: *Who cares! Feel lighter!*

MON 15 FEB

What a dream! Had Flexy-Lexy and Annie on my back as I did donkey calf raises like in *Pumping Iron* but they were ripping up *Spectator ONLY* tickets and laughing! The spell's broken!

About this time last year, two women were laughing at me but now it's with me. I did Flexy and Annie in one 24-hour period. That's technically a threesome.

2 a.m. Remembered Arnold's peak-moment metaphor. Now I can confirm it. The naughty atoms might even beat the quality atoms.

3 a.m. Quality atoms better. Don't have to nod or smile to get them.

TUE 16 FEB

It's crazy that Max hid his protein preference. How did he resist? Not being gay, but how did he resist me? All that time I thought he was taunting me but in reality I was taunting him. People say nothing online is real but he's proof that offline can be just as fake. Maybe the online world isn't a problem. Maybe it reflects life. My calves aren't ideal in any world.

WED 17 FEB

Was out for a think-walk and when I came back sister was leaving my room. Asked what she was doing and she said looking for more weights. Asked what happened to Wednesday "woga" and she went bright red. She won't admit I got her into the whole weights thing. Others may have fake followers online but I've got real life ones. That's not far off Jesus. Better calm down my rising confidence or people will celebrate my death with a cow's milk chocolate egg.

THU 18 FEB

The algorithm won't let me escape from Chad Showcracker PhD. Saw a video where he was talking about hormonal issues. Can't trust him on training so no idea why he should be trusted on this stuff. Him and another white coat were joking about "lasting longer". Then the algorithm steered me to "alpha" male videos, pick-up artists and their tips on prolonging pleasure. These guys have got it all wrong, everyone has, there's nothing manly about holding back.
    High-intensity works in everything.

FRI 19 FEB

First day of Pisces and it's made me bonkers. Got got a dirty mark! Reckon even York would smile.

TATTOOS
ARE
UGLY

SAT 20 FEB

The dirty mark is a source of new energy and now looking forward to showing a lucky lady. Got me thinking about Mitch Viola and watched him training and cruising for old time's sake. Won't go down his route of being splattered but appreciate his pain tolerance and have forgiven him for *8-hour arms*. Played the *Natty Anthem* for hours. Dad could have used it to become the envelope king.

2 a.m. Will cut out caffeine for a bit as getting loopy.

SUN 21 FEB

Wonder whether the girls would have yielded if I only weighed 10 dictionaries instead of 12? Probably just needed to take my shirt off and not sure I needed gear to do that.

I always assumed Annie was wild, yet despite all her muscle and macho (and slap) she was a kitten. Then Flexy, well I always thought she was prim and proper, and yet she turned out to be nothing but naughty. Appearances can be deceptive. As is someone in this house because my diary's been moved. Asked sister politely and she laughed. She will never get a boyfriend.

SUNDAY SUM-UP

The road back can begin with just remembering a time when things felt better.

- KAI GREENE

Weight: *11.9 dictionaries*

MON 22 FEB

Chad Showcracker PhD has a physique! Was rambling online and a pic of him came up without a shirt and he used to be muscular. He even competed. That'll teach me to judge a book by its lab coat. He doesn't look as good now though because being a boffin killed his gains. At least that confirms I was right to skip uni. From now on it's lift and let lift.

I take my hat off to you, Chad. But I still won't wear a baseball cap.

TUE 23 FEB

Had a caffeine-withdrawal headache at midday which got really bad. Brain thumped like high-rep squats. Going to bed ridiculously early.

11 p.m. Was asleep but thought dad was leaning over my pillow saying "Love yourself, don't wait." Woke up. Don't think I've heard him say it for ages. Did I imagine him saying it? Maybe I said it. Must sleep.

2 a.m. Woke up, watched *Makaveli Motivation*, felt like crying. Switched to Joe Rogan. Felt like kettlebells.

WED 24 FEB

People have slated me for living this lifestyle, family, friends, strangers, and yet they never give me any good reasons why, but instead just hate, and at times that really annoys me, hurts me, makes me doubt, and then I go online and look stuff up and realize there are others like me, doing the same, probably getting attacked and put-off all the same, but they still do it, and that's what keeps me going, because I know what I like pursuing, I know what I like doing, even if I don't really know why, I just do, and it warms me up to think that at any given moment of the night or day, someone out there is mixing a protein shake, spilling a protein shake, popping pills, stopping pills, trying a new exercise, trying another damn routine, reading stuff, hearing stuff, watching, living and breathing the same freaky fascinations I do, and I love it, probably always will, so hate away, because that's the way it's gonna be.

THU 25 FEB

170-word sentence. That's what happens when you suddenly stop studying. Or suddenly stop caffeine.

FRI 26 FEB

In the year I've been training I've changed a lot. But what hasn't changed much is the online fitness community. Sometimes there isn't much community because when I look at comments there's often some kind of divide.

But I've spotted an example of where opposite groups don't realize how similar they are. These groups are represented by two men. They're the two most important men in modern training, and neither's Arnold. Arnie's the most famous but he wasn't that different to what existed. He was better, yes, then got into movies.

These two men had different beliefs, different behaviors, and different goals. One was showy, one was shadowy. Yet underneath, their spirit glowed in similar ways.

The two men are Zyzz and Dorian. Before Zyzz there was no concept of training just for fun, for girls, for the lifestyle. And there was definitely no Fit-Fish whatever they say. Without Zyzz, online fitness might never have taken off.

Then there's Dorian. Before him there were big guys, there were cut guys, and there were guys with flow. People assumed you could only pick two of these characteristics. Dorian picked three. Before Dorian, this combo simply didn't exist.

If Zyzz was the "aesthetics movement" then Dorian was the "intensity movement". Zyzz and Dorian both defined the time before and after their rise. They defined eras. There's *before Zyzz* and there's *after Zyzz*. There's *before Dorian* and there's *after Dorian*. Both grabbed life by the scruff of its neck and did exactly what they wanted. Surely that's what we all dream of.

And whether you love them or hate them, you can't ignore them. They're true gamechangers. And if they can share common ground, I'm sure nattys and non-nattys can do the same.

SAT 27 FEB

Sister went mad at breakfast when I spilled OJ on her notepad. Said it was a "gratitude journal" but showed no gratitude when I laughed. Even said I should be more grateful considering how lucky I am. How lucky I am?

Went for a think-walk to calm down a bit and found a lucky coin. It had *STANDING ON THE SHOULDERS OF GIANTS* written on its edge. Isaac Newton said it. Realized I was grateful for resisting the gravity of his falling apple thousands of times. Helped me build shoulders that others will stand on.

SUN 28 FEB

Went by the electrical store for old time's sake. Got there but it was shut down. It's now dad's place, *Flights of Fancy.*

Came back home and went up into my room. Found a piece of white card on my bed. Had a *Post-it* note stuck on top with sister's writing:

> ~~A journey of a thousand miles begins with the first step~~
> A journey of 5000 miles begins with the last piece...

Peeled off note and saw a jigsaw piece glued to the card. It was the final missing bit from my 1000-piece *World Map*, a bit of the US.

Looked inside the card and saw weird digits.

Thought it was a coded insult until the 170 IQ ("107") kicked-in and I turned the card over to work it out.

> You had it all along.
> Don't forget the sun cream FWEDDY WILLY!
> Happy Birthday, love Lex and Dad.

I'M GOING TO LA TOMORROW!!!!!!

Sister had snuck into room for birthday ideas and found my diary. She quickly read the last 2 weeks and saw the Dorian seminar stuff. So her and dad did a cash collab and bought me a plane ticket (discounted) plus hotel. I take it back, *Flights of Fancy* is practical! Dad said the training, Tongkat, and help on envelopes gave him the confidence mother never did, plus he felt bad for me delaying uni.

God, I really love Sundays.

SUNDAY SUM-UP

They say don't put all your eggs in one basket.
But I only had one egg and one basket.
I put everything in to it.

- DORIAN YATES

Weight: *170 LBS!*
Scrapped dictionaries!
Soon to be weightless in a plane!

MON 29 FEB

5 a.m.   I'm up! Everyone's asleep and for once there isn't a crisis.

6.30   In Otis's taxi heading to airport. Mr Patel saw me leaving and rushed over to give me a gift. It's India's most famous book, the *Kama Sutra*. Glanced inside it and was shocked. No wonder India's got a billion people. Mr Patel said "Warrior or worrier?" Gave him a thumbs-up and said "Warrior" which made him smile. Then shouted I was going to the Mecca and his smile went. He must prefer yoga to bodybuilding. Otis has lost 20 kilos, the weight of my case. The cab didn't even lean on corners. Asked how he lost the chub and he said he just did it. Well, just stopped buying Manager Des's *Triple Threat*. Hugged at the drop-off zone and got my arms almost three-quarters around.

8 a.m.   Checked in. Didn't even squirm when I asked airport helper girl where *Virgin* desk was.

8.30   Did fragrance store but bought nothing as already wearing the cologne called *30 Pounds of Extra Muscle*.

9   On plane. Seat not designed for penthouse delts.

9.25   Pretty cabin crew girl smiled when showing emergency exits. She wants me to make an emergency entrance.

9.30   In the air! Energy crash. Hope the plane doesn't.

1 p.m.   About to be served lunch. Considered putting *Kama Sutra* on tray table to impress pretty cabin crew girl but played the long-game and did protein bar instead.

1.10   My side served by cabin crew male, just my luck! Pretty cabin crew girl must be intimidated. Don't blame her. Cabin crew male smiled at my bar. Hope it was the bar.

2.30   About to watch *Mission Impossible*. What's impossible, Tom?

1 p.m.   Landed in LA! The heat! The sky! Felt hyper so wrote my number on the cover of in-flight magazine. Added smiley. Left on tray. Pretty cabin crew girl could regain confidence.

1.05   Waiting for bags. Concerned male crew will get number.

2   At the *Marriot Marina Del Ray*, a mile from Venice Beach! Room's huge (space for three). Will change into t-shirt, shorts, and York's *Ultraboosts*.

3 p.m. GOLD'S GYM VENICE!!!

Signed in and strolled into the legendary Gold's Gym posing room.
Posing room, me! Must be a hundred times more mirrors than the
Fox-hole and way beyond covering with a towel. Took my shirt off,
stood square on, and posed. Two big dudes opened the door behind
me and asked how long I'd be. Said 5 minutes and didn't even reach
for *Nemo*. They nodded and left. Can't believe they actually thought 5
minutes of posing was ok. Can't believe I took 5. I stood in front of
the most competitive mirrors in the world. I stood in front of myself.

This time last year, if a psychic told me I'd skip uni but it would
turn out alright, I wouldn't have believed them. But here I am, maybe
I learned more. Plus I got the girl. Girls! And if they'd told me I'd
make a new friend, but that he'd be gone after a few months, I
wouldn't have believed that either. Yet I'm damn happy we met and
know you're up there smirking over the gym counter in the sky.

I won a show and even though they took back the sword I still kept
the memory of "First place, Freddy Fox". As for getting a bit of help,
so what. People get help in all areas, all day long, and now I know who
else has been naughty. And after all that's happened, I'm certain of
this, I'd rather be a half-natty than a full Bieber.

Now tomorrow's my birthday and I'm 5000 miles from home. What
should I do? What would Dorian do?

I know. I'll ask him in a minute...

HALF-NATTY

FREDDY FOX

Fellow double-layers,
Skip a session, skip a meal,
But show off today,
Don't wait, REVEAL!

Dear Mr Hastings, please reply to my thoughts about bringing *Netflix* to Korea.
Don't wait too long or I'll tell Mr Bezos. He's breast-fed and quite ambitious.

freddyfox@comic.com

Printed in Great Britain
by Amazon